*Samuel French Acting Edition*

I0584674

# Greater Clements

*by* Samuel D. Hunter

---

**FOR PRODUCTION ENQUIRIES**

UNITED STATES AND CANADA
info@concordtheatricals.com
1-866-979-0447

UNITED KINGDOM AND EUROPE
licensing@concordtheatricals.co.uk
020-7054-7200

Each title is subject to availability from Concord Theatricals Corp.,
depending upon country of performance. Please be aware that
*GREATER CLEMENTS* may not be licensed by Concord Theatricals
Corp. in your territory. Professional and amateur producers should
contact the nearest Concord Theatricals Corp. office or licensing
partner to verify availability.

---

be invented, including mechanical, electronic, photocopying, recording, videotaping, or otherwise, without the prior written permission of the publisher. No one shall upload this title(s), or part of this title(s), to any social media websites.

For all enquiries regarding motion picture, television, and other media rights, please contact Concord Theatricals Corp.

## MUSIC USE NOTE

Licensees are solely responsible for obtaining formal written permission from copyright owners to use copyrighted music in the performance of this play and are strongly cautioned to do so. If no such permission is obtained by the licensee, then the licensee must use only original music that the licensee owns and controls. Licensees are solely responsible and liable for all music clearances and shall indemnify the copyright owners of the play(s) and their licensing agent, Concord Theatricals Corp., against any costs, expenses, losses and liabilities arising from the use of music by licensees. Please contact the appropriate music licensing authority in your territory for the rights to any incidental music.

## IMPORTANT BILLING AND CREDIT REQUIREMENTS

If you have obtained performance rights to this title, please refer to your licensing agreement for important billing and credit requirements.

*GREATER CLEMENTS* was originally produced by Lincoln Center Theater (Andre Bishop, artistic director), premiering at the Newhouse Theater in New York City on November 14, 2019. The performance was directed by Davis McCallum, with sets by Dane Laffrey, costumes by Kaye Voyce, lighting by Yi Zhao, original music and sound by Fitz Patton, and dramaturgy by John M. Baker and Anne Cattaneo. The stage manager was Roxana Khan. The cast was as follows:

| | |
|---|---|
| **MAGGIE** | Judith Ivey |
| **JOE** | Edmund Donovan |
| **BILLY** | Ken Narasaki |
| **KEL** | Haley Sakamoto |
| **OLIVIA** | Nina Hellman |
| **WAYNE** | Andrew Garman |
| **MONA** | Kate MacCluggage |

*GREATER CLEMENTS* was developed at the Ojai Playwrights Conference (Robert Egan, artistic director/producer) and at the Lark Play Development Center in New York City.

# CHARACTERS

**MAGGIE** – female, 65, white

**JOE** – Maggie's son, 27, white

**BILLY** – male, 65, Japanese-American

**KEL** – Billy's granddaughter, 14, Japanese-American

**OLIVIA** – female, mid-forties

**WAYNE** – male, mid-fifties

**MONA** – female, mid-thirties


# SETTING

All scenes take place inside and immediately outside a small mine tour office and mining museum in a very small town in northern Idaho, with living space upstairs. The building itself has seen better days; it was constructed around the turn of the twentieth century, indicative of tiny Western towns with single-street downtowns that once had wood-plank sidewalks and hitching posts outside. The museum itself seems to be half-packed up – there are boxes around the space, many of the exhibits have been taken down, etc.

On the first level, there are store windows with posted hours and an open/close sign, with a front door that leads to a small reception area with posted tour prices, touristy knick-knacks for sale, etc. Somewhat out of place is a small shelf on which rests a pocket watch on a stand encased in a small bell jar. Past the reception area, the majority of the ground floor is a museum dedicated to a single mine called the Dodson Mine. There are several old maps, historic photos, examples of drill bits and axes and hammers from the turn of the twentieth century, etc. On the far wall, there is a door marked "Private" that leads to an office.

On the second level, stairs lead to a hallway that heads to an unseen bathroom and second bedroom. On one side of the hallway there is a modest bedroom, and on the other side there is a living room with an old, worn pull-out couch and a recliner. There is an unseen kitchen area off of the living room.

## AUTHOR'S NOTES

Dialogue written in *italics* is emphatic, deliberate; dialogue in ALL CAPS is impulsive, explosive. Dialogue in [brackets] is implied, not spoken.

A slash (/) indicates an overlap in dialogue. Whenever a slash appears, the following line of dialogue should begin.

Ellipses (...) indicate when a character is trailing off. Dashes (–) indicate where a character is being cut off, either by another character or themself.

# ACT ONE

## Scene One

*(Complete darkness. Then, a single light comes on. We see that it's emanating from a miner's helmet on top of* **JOE**'s *head.)*

*(A silence as* **JOE** *looks over the audience. Finally:)*

**JOE.** Here we're at a depth of about twenty-five hundred feet, or about half a mile. The elevator here goes down another four thousand feet, off of which are about thirty-four different shafts. And you can feel that it's getting warmer – it gets hotter and hotter as you go down. Once you hit six thousand feet, the temperature is in excess of a-hundred and fifteen degrees. Mine was operational until twelve years ago, shut down the summer of 2005. When it closed, base pay was nine dollars and fifteen cents an hour. The minerals that were mined here at Dodson Mine were silver, lead, zinc, copper, little bit of gold, some molybdenum... Oh – I have a joke.

*(Short pause.)*

Guy falls down into the mine. His boss hears him hit the ground and he shouts, "Did you break anything?" The guy answers back, "Just rocks down here, sir, nothing to break."

*(Pause, smiling.)*

That's my joke.

*(Short pause.)*

**JOE.** Oh, and keep in mind, these miners had very little light to work off of. Only this.

> *(He points to his helmet light.)*

And before that...

> *(He switches off his helmet light. We're in total darkness. After a moment, **JOE** strikes a lighter. We can barely make out his face.)*

Back in the late 1800s, this is all they had. Weirdly enough though, the big fire happened long after they started using headlamps. 1972. Eighty-one dead. Fire started all the way down at the bottom, sixty-four-hundred level. My grandfather, Robert Bunker, burned alive that day. On the sixty-four-hundred level, where it started. All the way down.

> *(Pause.)*

These elevators here go down there. Over a mile into the surface of the earth. County said we're not allowed to take people all the way down, the tunnels aren't reliable, way too hot.

> *(Pause.)*

But I guess –... I might not get the chance again.

> *(The flame goes out.)*

> *(In the darkness, we hear the sound of something shattering. Lights come up on the space, revealing:)*

## Scene Two

> (**MAGGIE** *is on the ground floor, near the front register, holding a duster. She is looking down at the floor – the pocket watch and the bell jar covering it have fallen off the shelf; the bell jar has shattered.* **MAGGIE** *has a portable phone pressed to her ear.*)

**MAGGIE.** *Shit.*

> (*Pause, on the phone.*)

No, I'm fine, I just –... I just knocked over something, it's fine.

> (*She picks up the watch, looking at it. The crystal is slightly broken. She listens.*)

Well listen, Livvy, I just don't know if I care anymore, the whole town's been talking about it for months now, I'm just sort of sick of it, I –... Livvy, can you hear me?

> (*Pause.*)

*Dammit.*

> (*She takes the phone away from her ear, hitting the back of it a few times. She puts the phone back to her ear.*)

Livvy?!

> (*She doesn't hear anything. She does the same thing again, puts the phone back to her ear.*)

You there?!

> (*Pause.*)

Okay, I can hear you now.

> (*Short pause.*)

Well if it's that annoying then buy me a new phone why don't you.

> (*Silence, she listens.*)

**MAGGIE.** I guess it just doesn't matter to me, with the mine shut down it was only a matter of time before I closed up shop, so it's not a big deal to me, it's –... Well, sure.

> *(Silence. She listens.)*

> *(Then, from outside, we begin to hear a voice approaching the front door. It's inaudible at first, becoming more and more discernible as* **OLIVIA** *reaches the door and opens it.)*

**OLIVIA.** ...Has been around since the mid-1800s, and I just think there's something to be said for town history, or town pride, or whatever you want to call it –

> *(She comes in through the front door, on her cell phone.)*

*(Without skipping a beat.)* – and I think that maybe people have forgotten about that!

> *(***OLIVIA*** and* **MAGGIE** *hang up their phones.)*

**MAGGIE.** Well, I just don't care that much about it all at this point.

**OLIVIA.** Oh c'mon, you're just being callous now.

**MAGGIE.** "Callous"?! Where'd you get that word? You hear that from Cynthia, / is that where you got that?

**OLIVIA.** You know this means they're not going to do any more curbside garbage pick-ups.

**MAGGIE.** Oh I go to the dump once a week anyway. And they never took recycling so I've always had / to do that myself –

**OLIVIA.** They won't have people snow-blowing your sidewalk out there in the winter.

**MAGGIE.** I do that myself too!

**OLIVIA.** I don't understand why you're not more upset about this! You know a lot of people were pretty miffed that you didn't have a "No on 42" sign up in your window.

**MAGGIE.** Someone said something? Who said something?

**OLIVIA.** I don't know, people talk! The Floyds stopped going to the Lodge Café when they realized Henry was voting yes.

**MAGGIE**. Oh, the Lloyds are a bunch / of loudmouths.

**OLIVIA**. *Floyds* I said.

**MAGGIE**. They're even worse!

**OLIVIA**. Others feel the same way. Henry says he probably lost a lot of business.

**MAGGIE**. Well I'm closing this place anyway, so it doesn't matter if I lose business. Did you want these maps, by the way?

**OLIVIA**. Hm?

**MAGGIE**. I thought you said something about wanting these old mine maps, here.

> *(She points to some old, turn-of-the-century mining maps.)*

**OLIVIA**. I just said I *liked* them. You don't want to save those? I thought they were your dad's.

**MAGGIE**. Granddad's, actually. I don't care, they're just old maps.

> *(She grabs a dustbuster from behind the counter, approaches area where the watch fell.)*
>
> *(***JOE*** appears in the upstairs hallway, having just woken up. He makes his way into the living room, heading toward the kitchen area.)*

**OLIVIA**. I'm just surprised you're okay with this.

**MAGGIE**. I'm not even sure what it all means! And I don't know, if this is a way to stick it to those California people, then I'm fine with that.

> *(She turns on the dustbuster. They have to shout over the noise.)*
>
> *(Upstairs, ***JOE*** disappears into the kitchen area.)*

**OLIVIA**. But this is where our families grew up! Generations / of –!

**MAGGIE**. You know what? I'm done talking about this. Go over to Cynthia's if you wanna talk to somebody about it, it's all she ever talks about.

(*She turns off the dustbuster.*)

**MAGGIE.** (*Re: the dustbuster.*) Well this isn't helping at all.

    (*She reaches down, picking up the glass left behind by the dustbuster.*)

    (**OLIVIA** *goes to her.*)

**OLIVIA.** What was it?

**MAGGIE.** Oh, the –. My dad's old pocket watch. I knocked it over, the bell jar it was in shattered. Cracked the crystal on the watch a little bit. Maybe Joe won't notice.

    (*There's a silence as she picks up the glass shards off the floor.*)

    (*Upstairs,* **JOE** *returns from the kitchen area, eating a banana. He sits down on the couch.*)

**OLIVIA.** Joe's still doing – okay?

**MAGGIE.** *Yes,* Livvy, he's –. He's just upstairs, he's fine.

**OLIVIA.** That's good, I just –.

    (**MAGGIE** *looks away.* **JOE** *stops eating the banana, staring forward.*)

    (*Pause.*)

So – has he decided if he's back here for good?

    (*Pause.*)

**MAGGIE.** He's home, that's where we are right now. I brought him home. It's good.

**OLIVIA.** Well that's for certain! That's definitely – for certain.

    (**MAGGIE** *looks at her. Tense pause.* **OLIVIA** *heads for a coffee maker.*)

You have coffee?

**MAGGIE.** You can make some if you want.

**OLIVIA.** I can just do the instant.

**MAGGIE.** You can make a pot if you want, it'll get drunk.

    (**OLIVIA** *plugs an electric kettle into the wall.*)

**OLIVIA.** Anyway, I just think it's sad is all I'm saying. Clements was such a great town to grow up in. My dad used to leave the keys to his pickup in the ignition, couldn't even walk down the street without seeing a relative. I crocheted that blanket for the centennial, you remember that?

**MAGGIE.** Sure, ugly thing.

**OLIVIA.** I did it to raise money for / the mobile library!

**MAGGIE.** I didn't say it wasn't *nice* of you, I just said it was ugly.

**OLIVIA.** Now I don't even know what to call myself. Where the heck am I supposed to say that I live?

**MAGGIE.** Fred Eskelin was saying we should just say we live in Silver County.

**OLIVIA.** Well sure, but how do we call ourselves? "Silverites"? That doesn't sound right at all.

**MAGGIE.** Since when did you call yourself a "Clementine"? *Dammit.*

>  *(She has cut her finger on a shard of glass.)*

Livvy, look what you made me do.

**OLIVIA.** How was that my fault?!

**MAGGIE.** That smarts. Gimme a minute.

>  *(She makes her way offstage to the office.)*

**OLIVIA.** I'm sorry! Wasn't my fault, but sorry!

>  *(**MAGGIE** exits.)*

>  *(**OLIVIA** turns to the coffee, waiting for the water to boil. She checks it, then opens up a cupboard, looking for instant coffee.)*

>  *(**JOE** leaves the living room and descends the stairs. **OLIVIA** doesn't notice him. **JOE** looks around the room. He immediately notices that the pocket watch is broken. He goes to the shelf, looking up.)*

(*OLIVIA finds the instant coffee, pours a little bit into a mug. She pulls out a spoon.*)

**JOE.** What / happened to the –?

(*OLIVIA lets out a little shriek, whipping around.*)

**OLIVIA.** Oh my God, Joe –

**JOE.** Sorry! Sorry.

**OLIVIA.** It's fine, I just didn't hear you!

**JOE.** Sorry, Mrs. Brown.

**OLIVIA.** I told you, call me Livvy. You're an adult now.

**JOE.** Okay.

(*Awkward silence.* **OLIVIA** *forces a smile.*)

Do you know what happened to the watch?

**OLIVIA.** Oh, I –. I think your mom was cleaning, I think she knocked it over or something.

(**JOE** *picks up the watch, looking at it.*)

It's still okay, just a little broken on the face there.

(**JOE** *continues to look at the watch.*)

(*Silence. Finally,* **OLIVIA** *struggles to make conversation.*)

It's just such a shame that this place has to shut down like this!

(*Pause.* **JOE** *looks at her.*)

**JOE.** Yeah, / it's –

**OLIVIA.** You were so good at doing those mine tours. I still remember how animated you were, I remember thinking to myself – that boy is going to be an actor someday.

**JOE.** Really? You thought I'd be an actor?

**OLIVIA.** Or maybe a game show host! Something like that. You were just so animated! And even when you were little. When I'd babysit you, you'd take me all around the museum here.

(**JOE** *looks around the museum for a moment, lost in thought.* **OLIVIA** *watches him.*)

So, now that this place is shutting down... Have you given any more thought to – what you're gonna *do* here?

(*Short pause.*)

**JOE**. I... No, not really.

(*Pause.*)

**OLIVIA**. 'Cause you know, your mom isn't a young woman anymore.

(**JOE** *looks at her.* **MAGGIE** *re-enters from the office with a Band-Aid on the tip of her finger. She sees* **OLIVIA** *with* **JOE**.)

**MAGGIE**. Oh –

**OLIVIA**. We're okay! / We're fine.

**JOE**. What happened to the watch?

(*Pause.* **MAGGIE** *looks at him.*)

**MAGGIE**. I was cleaning, it was an accident. There's no use in getting upset –

**JOE**. I'm not upset, / Mom –

**MAGGIE**. Okay, I'm just saying.

(*Pause.* **JOE** *puts the watch back on the shelf.*)

You want something to eat? I didn't finish my Lean Cuisine, it's on the counter there.

**JOE**. What is it?

**MAGGIE**. Lasagna.

**JOE**. You sure you don't want it?

**MAGGIE**. No, it tastes like cardboard. Have it.

(**JOE** *goes to the counter, starts eating the leftover lasagna.*)

Joe why don't you –? Have you asked Livvy how she's doing?

*(JOE looks at OLIVIA.)*

**JOE.** So how are you doing, Mrs. Brown? Livvy.

**OLIVIA.** I'm good! I did my pottery class last night. I've been taking this pottery class at the community center in Coeur d'Alene? Don't know what possessed me to do it but now I got all these pots. You want a pot?

**JOE.** Sure.

**OLIVIA.** Okay I'll bring you a pot then.

> *(Pause. The electric kettle whistles. OLIVIA goes to it, makes a cup of instant coffee.)*

**JOE.** You have cats, right? How are your cats?

**OLIVIA.** They've both been gone for a while now. Iggy died just last year if you can believe that. Nineteen years old, I swear to you.

**JOE.** What about Cat Cat?

**OLIVIA.** Oh he died ages ago, you were still in high school then.

**JOE.** Really? He was the black one, right?

**MAGGIE.** / Yeah, that's it.

**OLIVIA.** That's right. Ran out into the road, got hit by a truck. The driver was this gigantic logger or something, I think he was more upset about it than I was.

**JOE.** How's Cam?

> *(Pause. OLIVIA and MAGGIE tense up a bit.)*

**OLIVIA.** He's – good. Classes are going good. He likes this new dorm a lot better.

**JOE.** Oh, that's good.

**OLIVIA.** He's thinking of transferring into the Forestry program. *Really* good program, real good.

> *(Tense pause. JOE continues to eat the lasagna.)*

**MAGGIE.** Livvy, I know I keep saying this – but Joe really would love the opportunity to tell Cam he's sorry in person. Right, Joe?

> *(She looks at JOE. Pause.)*

**JOE**. Yeah, sure.

>(**OLIVIA** *looks away.*)

**OLIVIA**. Sure, maybe. Maggie, you said you had some old picture frames back in the office you were trying to give away, right? Why don't you show those to me.

>(*Pause.*)

**MAGGIE**. Yeah, I –. Okay.

>(*She exits into the office,* **OLIVIA** *follows.* **MAGGIE** *closes the door.*)

>(**JOE** *eats his lasagna, wandering around the space a bit. He looks up at the pocket watch. Just then,* **BILLY** *appears at the front door, followed by* **KEL**. *They come inside.*)

**BILLY**. Oh – hi there –

**JOE**. Hi, come on in!

**BILLY**. Thanks –

**JOE**. If you wanted a tour, we're actually not doing those / anymore –

**BILLY**. Oh no, we're – I'm an old friend of Maggie's? I called her a couple days ago, told her I'd be passing through town, she offered her pull-out couch –

**JOE**. Oh, right – she said you were coming later today –

**BILLY**. We ended up leaving pretty early –

**KEL**. I told you we got up at five in the morning for *no reason.*

**JOE**. My mom's right in back there, I can go get her if you –

**BILLY**. Are you –? You're Joe?

**JOE**. Yeah.

>(**KEL** *starts wandering around the space, looking at the exhibits.*)

**BILLY**. Oh, wow, I –. I met you once, you couldn't have been six years old, I –... I went to high school with your mom, down in Carmike Falls.

**JOE**. Oh.

**KEL.** What is this place, anyway?

    *(JOE immediately engages KEL.)*

**JOE.** Museum of the historic Dodson Mine, the largest mine in Idaho and one of the oldest and deepest mines in the country.

**KEL.** Oh.

    *(Short pause.)*

Grandpa, I'm just gonna go for a walk.

**BILLY.** Kel, I don't know / if –

**KEL.** I won't go far.

**JOE.** *(To KEL.)* I could show you the outside of the mine if you want. We can't go down but I can show you the top.

**BILLY.** Oh we don't want to trouble you –

**JOE.** No trouble at all. The entrance isn't far up the mountain at all, ten-minute walk, tops.

    *(Short pause.)*

I'm a really good tour guide.

    *(Pause. KEL shrugs.)*

**BILLY.** Okay, Kel, go on ahead. You have your phone, right?

**KEL.** Yeah.

    *(She heads to the door with JOE.)*

**JOE.** My mom's just in the back room there, go ahead on in.

**BILLY.** Oh, okay. Uh –.

    *(KEL and JOE leave. BILLY is left alone. He looks at the door to the back room.)*

    *(He paces around the space for a moment, anxious, unsure of what to do.)*

    *(He glances through exhibits, spotting one in particular. Underneath it is a large green button. He absentmindedly hits the button.)*

    *(Maggie's pre-recorded voice starts playing, a bit too loud.)*

**MAGGIE'S VOICE**. Each day, miners had to get rid of the excess rocks from the day before.

> (**BILLY** *winces at the volume, unsure of what to do.*)

They then had to make it safe overhead and on the sides for at least six feet of clearance. They then had to drill another round, and load it with explosives. If miners failed to –

> (**BILLY** *hits the button again, trying to make it stop. It restarts.*)

Each day, miners had to get rid of the excess rocks from the day before.

> (**MAGGIE** *comes out of the office.*)

**MAGGIE**. Joe, don't play with the –

> (*She closes the door behind her, then finally sees* **BILLY**. *They stare at one another.*)

**MAGGIE'S VOICE**. They then had to make it safe overhead and on the sides for at least six feet of clearance. They then had to drill another round, and load it with –

> (*Finally,* **MAGGIE** *goes behind the reception desk and unplugs something. The recording stops. They stare at each other. Pause.*)

**BILLY**. Hi, Maggie.

> (**OLIVIA** *enters from the back office, holding a couple of old frames.*)

**OLIVIA**. What about these two? They're kinda weird-looking, but I think they're okay for my front hall. (*Seeing* **BILLY**.) Oh, 'scuse me, I –

> (*Short pause.* **OLIVIA** *takes a longer look at* **BILLY**, *realizing.*)

Oh –

**MAGGIE**. Those frames are fine to take, Livvy.

**OLIVIA**. (*To* **BILLY**.) Wait... Are you –?

MAGGIE. *I'll see you tomorrow, Livvy.*

> (**OLIVIA** *pauses for a moment, giving* **MAGGIE** *a shocked look.*)

OLIVIA. Okay then, I'll –...

> (*She finally exits with the frames.*)

> (*Silence.* **BILLY** *and* **MAGGIE** *stare at one another.*)

MAGGIE. You're early.

BILLY. We left early, I was –. I was excited.

> (*Pause.*)

MAGGIE. You're actually here.

BILLY. I'm actually here.

> (**MAGGIE** *smiles. Pause.*)

> (**JOE** *and* **KEL** *re-enter.*)

JOE. *(To* **BILLY**.*)* Sorry, we had to turn back, sheriff drove by right as we were heading out. He's always following me around, he would've...

> (*He looks at* **MAGGIE**. *Pause.*)

What?

## Scene Three

(**JOE, MAGGIE, KEL,** *and* **BILLY** *are all upstairs in the living room. There's an open pizza box on the coffee table.* **JOE** *is looking through an old yearbook,* **MAGGIE** *stands over him.* **BILLY** *and* **MAGGIE** *are drinking beers.*)

**MAGGIE.** *(Pointing.)* That's me, there. I was on the swim team –

**BILLY.** Your mother was / quite the swimmer.

**MAGGIE.** – And I don't know if you remember the woman, this woman named Dottie? She came into town, did the mine tour, you remember that?

**JOE.** / I don't know...

**BILLY.** She came here through town? When was that?

**MAGGIE.** Oh it was a while ago, Joe was young. Anyway she was my swim coach. How is Dottie?

**BILLY.** Well that's the thing –

**KEL.** She's dead.

**MAGGIE.** Oh. I didn't even know she was sick.

**KEL.** She wasn't. Car accident outside of town, a semi tipped over on the highway toward Payette, crushed the whole / front half of her car –

**BILLY.** Okay, Kel, okay.

**KEL.** I'm just saying what happened.

**BILLY.** We're eating, hon.

**JOE.** Same thing happened to a friend of mine up in Alaska.

**KEL.** Really?

**JOE.** Yeah. But that was a Winnebago.

**MAGGIE.** / Okay, Joe, let's not –

**KEL.** What's that?

**JOE.** It's like a big RV? He was biking on the highway and a gust of wind / knocked over this Winnebago right as he was –

**MAGGIE.** Okay, Joe, that's enough!

*(Pause.)*

**MAGGIE.** Anyway, I was on the swim team.

*(**JOE** continues to flip through the yearbook.)*

**JOE.** *(To **MAGGIE**.)* How long did you and Grandpa and Grandma live in Carmike Falls?

**MAGGIE.** Oh my dad got a job teaching at the heavy machinery school when I was in the – sixth grade?

**BILLY.** Fifth. I remember, we were both in the fifth grade. Mrs. Arnold.

**MAGGIE.** My senior year we moved back up here, my dad started working at the mine again.

**JOE.** Why did he leave the heavy machinery school?

**MAGGIE.** Oh I don't think he ever liked working there, he... *(Looking at the yearbook.)* There he is! Billy, that's you!

*(**BILLY** looks at the photo.)*

**BILLY.** Haven't aged a day, have I?
*(Pointing at the yearbook.)* Oh – and there's our prom. Senior prom.

**JOE.** You guys went together?

**MAGGIE.** Sure.

**BILLY.** Oh and there's Cindy Hashimoto, you remember Cindy Hashimoto?

**MAGGIE.** Oh, yeah.

**JOE.** There were a lot of...

*(**MAGGIE** and **BILLY** look at **JOE**. Short pause.)*

I mean for a little town in Idaho? There were a lot of Asian kids in your class.

**MAGGIE.** Oh yeah, we had a lot of Japanese families in Carmike Falls, a lot of kids in our class. Megan Etsuko, Jamie Amano, Greg Sunada –

**BILLY.** Charles Tanaka.

**MAGGIE.** Oh Lord, Charles Tanaka, who could forget that weird bird?

*(**MAGGIE** and **BILLY** laugh. Pause.)*

**BILLY**. You really sure you wanna take us in this weekend? We can easily grab a motel room –

**MAGGIE**. No, we've got room! I mean if you don't mind sharing the pull-out here.

(*She indicates the couch.*)

**BILLY**. That's just fine.

**MAGGIE**. Oh and how's Patrick doing? Last time I saw him, he was probably nine or ten years old.

**BILLY**. He's okay, he's – working through some stuff. Kel's staying with me for the time being.

**KEL**. Can I just go read my book in the car?

**BILLY**. Oh hon, I don't know, it's kinda late to be wandering around outside –

**KEL**. I'm *really* bored.

**BILLY**. Kel, / don't be rude.

**JOE**. I can show you around the museum downstairs if you want.

(*Short pause.* **KEL** *shrugs.*)

**KEL**. Yeah, okay.

(**JOE** *gets up, starts heading toward the stairs with* **KEL**.)

**MAGGIE**. Joe, you –... You're just going downstairs, right?

(**JOE** *stops, looks at* **MAGGIE**.)

**JOE**. Yes, Mom, I –. I'm just gonna show her around the museum. We'll be right downstairs.

**MAGGIE**. Okay then.

(*She smiles at* **JOE**. **JOE** *and* **KEL** *head into the museum.* **BILLY** *and* **MAGGIE** *are left alone together. Pause.*)

I – heard Sue passed.

**BILLY**. She did. Three years ago now.

**MAGGIE**. Three?! That long ago? My God, that's...

**BILLY**. I should have called, or written you. I didn't know what to say.

(*Pause.*)

**MAGGIE**. How did [she die]...?

**BILLY**. She had a stroke.

**MAGGIE**. A stroke?! At her age?!

**BILLY**. Fifty-seven. Young.

**MAGGIE**. My God. I'm so sorry, Billy.

**BILLY**. It was sudden. She didn't suffer.

**MAGGIE**. Sure.

(*Short pause.*)

I'm just gonna...

(*Anxious, she gets up and takes some paper plates into the kitchen area.*)

(*Downstairs,* **KEL** *looks at an exhibit, reading.*)

**JOE**. (*Pointing.*) This ore here was mined from Dodson in the 1920s, it's a mix of silver, gold, and pyrite, which you may know as "fool's gold" because of its / similarity to –

**KEL**. I can read.

(*She wanders to another exhibit, away from* **JOE**.)

**JOE**. Oh. Okay.

(**KEL** *spots something.*)

**KEL**. (*Pointing to an exhibit.*) Wait – what's this?

**JOE**. 1972 fire. One of the worst disasters in mining history. Eighty-one people dead.

**KEL**. *Woah*, really?

(*She reads with great interest.* **JOE** *watches her.*)

(**MAGGIE** *comes back into the living room.*)

(*Silence.*)

**MAGGIE**. So, you –...? The cancer, it's –?

**BILLY**. Not a big deal. I beat it once, I can beat it again.

**MAGGIE**. But I mean – is it worse this time, or –?

**BILLY**. I can handle it, Maggie. I promise.

>  *(Pause.)*

**MAGGIE**. Does Kel know?

**BILLY**. She doesn't need to know, she's going through enough right now.

>  *(Pause.)*

After Sue passed, I meant to call you. But it just – took some getting used to, life without her. And her death hit Patrick hard, he –... Anyway, I needed to spend some time to make sure that Kel was okay.

**MAGGIE**. Sure.

**BILLY**. But last week, when I got the diagnosis... Suddenly, it was like – what the hell am I waiting for? Life is too short, it's –...

>  *(Pause. **MAGGIE** nervously looks away.)*

**MAGGIE**. You want anything else?

**BILLY**. No, I...

>  (**MAGGIE**, *still anxious, closes the pizza box, taking it into the kitchen.)*

**KEL**. Wait, so if the fire started all the way at the bottom –

**JOE**. Sixty-four-hundred level.

**KEL**. Whatever. But why did people die who were only halfway down?

**JOE**. Smoke inhalation and toxic gas.

>  *(He shows **KEL** a map of the mine.)*

>  *(Pointing.)* When crews went to rescue them, the hoists stopped working on the thirty-four-hundred level here and they had to go down to the four-thousand level, then they had to use the consil line to get to the shafts full of gas. By then everyone was dead. Bodies here –
>  *(Pointing.)* Here –
>  *(Pointing.)* And a *bunch* more here.

**KEL**. *Woah*. Did they shut down the mine after that?

**JOE**. No it didn't shut down until 2005. They reopened the mine about two months after the fire.

**KEL**. *Two months?!* That's so crazy, like – all of these people who had been working there just went back to work in, like, the exact same shafts where they cleared out a bunch of their friends' corpses a couple / months before –

**JOE**. I mean – it's not just some fun story. People died. My grandpa died down there.

**KEL**. Seriously? Where?

**JOE**. Sixty-four-hundred line.

**KEL**. *Woah*. Where the fire started?

**JOE**. Yeah.

> *(Pointing.)* You see this watch?

>> *(He grabs the pocket watch off the shelf, handing it to* **KEL**.*)*

> This was my grandpa's, it's the only thing we have left of him. He had it with him when he died in the fire.

**KEL**. *Wow.*

**JOE**. He carried it all the time I guess, got it in the war. It's like a miracle that it survived the fire.

**KEL**. He "got it in the war"?

**JOE**. Yeah, World War II. Took it off a dead soldier.

>> *(Pause.)*

**KEL**. Oh.

>> *(She hands the watch to* **JOE**. **JOE** *puts it back on the shelf.)*

>> *(Pause.)*

**JOE**. You wanna see something?

**KEL**. What?

>> *(***JOE*** goes into the office, turning on the light.* **KEL** *follows him.)*

>> *(Upstairs,* **MAGGIE** *comes back into the living room with* **BILLY**.*)*

**BILLY**. I heard that – Caleb wasn't around anymore.

**MAGGIE**. Left a long time ago. He's living with this friend of his down in Boise.

**BILLY**. Oh.

*(Pause.)*

**MAGGIE**. He's gay, you know. That's what happened.

**BILLY**. Oh, I – I didn't know that.

**MAGGIE**. I mean I always knew something was wrong with him, I –. I mean not *wrong*, I don't mean… I knew that something was *going on* with him, that's what I mean to say. But honestly, I had no idea. All came to a head when Joe was in junior high. We had just gotten the internet. I had no idea it was going on until I walked in one night, he was on the computer, and I just casually asked him what he was looking at and he broke down, told me everything. He met a man, he's very nice, they live together now down in Boise. He's got a lot of friends.

**BILLY**. Oh.

**MAGGIE**. I mean I'm happy for him! I'm glad he could, you know. Find himself. 'Course he got to find himself, and meanwhile I was left raising a fourteen-year-old by myself.

*(Downstairs, **KEL** exits the office, followed by* **JOE**.*)*

**KEL**. Those are *amazing*.

**JOE**. I know, right?

**KEL**. Why aren't those in the museum?

**JOE**. My mom doesn't like them.

*(**JOE** and **KEL** start to slowly head back upstairs.)*

**MAGGIE**. I thought about calling. After Caleb left. Thought maybe that was the now or never moment.

**BILLY**. Had a lot of those moments over the years. Wasn't sure about any of them.

*(Pause.)*

**BILLY**. I sold the farm a while back, just after Sue died. Used the money to buy myself a little place closer to town. On this ridge that overlooks the river. It's not fancy but it's – nice. I – think you'd like it.

*(Short pause.)*

**MAGGIE**. You're asking if I'd –?

**BILLY**. I know this isn't exactly the most romantic version of all this, all these years later and me being sick, and –. But I've got time left. Maybe even a long time. And it could be really – nice. You know?

**MAGGIE**. Yeah, I –...

*(Pause. She looks down.)*

**BILLY**. What?

> *(**KEL** arrives in the living room, followed by **JOE**. **MAGGIE** stops herself.)*

**MAGGIE**. Oh. You're back.

**BILLY**. You learn neat things about the mine?

**JOE**. She liked the story of the big 1972 fire.

**BILLY**. Oh, sure.

**KEL**. *(To **BILLY**.)* Did you know that *eighty-one* people died down there?

**BILLY**. *(To **MAGGIE**.)* She likes ghost stories.

**KEL**. It's not a "ghost" story. Joe showed me old photographs from the fire, all these corpses they were bringing out of the mine that / were –

**MAGGIE**. Wait, Joe, you –? You showed her those?

**JOE**. She liked them.

**MAGGIE**. She's a child! What are you thinking?!

**BILLY**. Oh, it's okay. She's looked up worse than that on her phone, I promise you that.
*(Grabbing the yearbook.)* Mags, whatever happened to Boyd? Do you hear from him ever?

**MAGGIE**. He moved up to / Sandpoint, years ago. Was it Sandpoint?

**KEL**. *(To* **JOE**.*)* How long have you been doing the mine tours?

**MAGGIE**. *(Grabbing her beer.)* / Anyway, I haven't heard from him.

**JOE**. Before I left town, I did them all the time. Sometimes more than one a day.

**MAGGIE**. / What about George Campbell, how's he doing?

**KEL**. When did you leave town?

**JOE**. / Couple years after I graduated high school. Like seven years ago.

**BILLY**. He's still in town, he's around. I don't really see him anymore.

**KEL**. Where'd you go?

**JOE**. / To Alaska. I crashed in Anchorage for a while.

**MAGGIE**. I thought you and George were close.

**KEL**. / I wanna go to Alaska so bad. Did you love it?

**BILLY**. We were, we were. We just –...

**JOE**. / I mean it was really beautiful, Anchorage is a cool town. But it was all kind of a blur. It wasn't the best time for me.

**BILLY**. I don't know, these days we don't really talk as much as we used to. The Japanese families sort of keep to themselves.

**KEL**. / What do you mean?

**MAGGIE**. Oh. I didn't realize that.

**JOE**. / I have these issues. But they're under control now, so I'm better.

**BILLY**. Yeah just sort of happened gradually. Not sure why, just happened.

**KEL**. / Is it okay that I'm asking about it?

**MAGGIE**. I guess I remember it being like that, growing up.

**JOE**. / It's fine, I have this doctor now. She actually says it would be good for me to talk about it more.

**MAGGIE**. I never saw your parents in town, never saw them at the movies, restaurants. Or the fiddling festival.

**KEL.** / Were you on drugs? You can tell me, you don't need to treat me like I'm a little kid or anything.

**BILLY.** They kept to themselves, all our parents did. Guess we're all just turning into our parents.

**JOE.** No, it wasn't that. I mean mostly not. There was a little bit of drugs.

(**MAGGIE** *looks at* **JOE.**)

**MAGGIE.** What the heck are you two talking about?

**JOE.** Nothing.

**BILLY.** *(To* **MAGGIE,** *re: beer.)* You mind if I grab another?

**MAGGIE.** You stay here, I'll get it. Joe, Kel, you guys need anything?

**JOE.** / No.

**KEL.** I'm fine.

(**MAGGIE** *exits to get a beer.*)

Wait so what was going on?

**JOE.** After I graduated high school, things just started to get a little weird. And I just started feeling like I needed to get out of town.

**BILLY.** What's this?

**KEL.** Joe lived in Anchorage for a while.

**BILLY.** Oh, that's neat. I've been to Anchorage.

**JOE.** Yeah, it wasn't really like... It was okay at first, a guy I knew from high school was working at this salmon cannery, he got me a job there, it was okay. But I mean it wasn't like – totally my choice, I sorta had to get out of town for a while, I...

*(Pause. He looks away.)*

**KEL.** What?

**JOE.** I'm not sure if my mom wants me talking about it.

*(Pause.)*

Like a year or so after I graduated high school, I was working here, also doing some shifts at the Lodge Café, it was okay. But then I started having trouble seeing people's faces.

**KEL**. What do you mean?

**JOE**. Like every time I looked at people, they had duck faces.

> (**KEL** *giggles.*)

It's not funny.

**BILLY**. Kel.

**KEL**. Sorry, I'm not... What do you mean?

> (**MAGGIE** *re-enters with two more beers. She gives one to* **BILLY**.)

**JOE**. Like every time I would look at other people, I wouldn't see a face. I would see their eyes, but then the rest of their face below their eyes was like this long, weird thing of flesh and –

**MAGGIE**. Joe, what are you doing?

**JOE**. She asked me, I'm telling them because she asked me.

**MAGGIE**. I don't know if / we wanna –

**JOE**. Mom, she asked me! Dr. Carl says I'm supposed to be able to talk about this.

**KEL**. I asked him Mrs. Bunker.

> (*Pause.* **MAGGIE** *relents.*)

**JOE**. *Anyway.* I would see people's eyes, but then below that it just looked like their whole face was just this weird U-shape of flesh hanging down, no nose, no mouth. And then after a while I stopped seeing people's eyes, they were just like these two little black holes, I couldn't tell if people were looking at me or not. Only person who looked normal was my reflection in the mirror. I didn't know how to even talk about it back then, I couldn't look at people long enough to try and explain. My psychiatrist says it would help me to name it, to make it less scary. So now I say that I saw duck faces. Everyone had a duck face. So I was just surrounded by all these – things – that weren't human, they just had human voices, and I didn't trust them, and they always seemed to be coming at me, and Olivia's kid Cam used to ride his bike around town, and / this one time –

**MAGGIE.** *(Getting up.)* All right, I think that's enough, Joe.

**JOE.** I don't want to be *ashamed* of this stuff –

**MAGGIE.** I'm not saying you have to be ashamed of it! But maybe not everyone wants to hear about it, it makes some people uncomfortable!

**JOE.** / But she was asking about it!

**KEL.** I didn't mean / to...

**BILLY.** *(Trying to change the subject.)* I went up to Anchorage once. Beautiful town. Cold though, it was cold.

*(Short pause.)*

Real beautiful.

*(Tense silence. Finally, **MAGGIE** gets up.)*

**MAGGIE.** I'm gonna turn in pretty soon, I'll grab you the sheets and the pillows for the pull-out.

*(She exits briefly. Pause.)*

**JOE.** I wasn't trying to make anyone uncomfortable.

**KEL.** You weren't making me / uncomfortable.

**BILLY.** Okay, guys. Just leave it.

*(**MAGGIE** re-enters with sheets and pillows and heads toward the couch, starting to take off the cushions.)*

**MAGGIE.** It's got this bar in the middle that can be a little annoying during the night –

**JOE.** Mom.

**MAGGIE.** – There's a sheet of particle board behind the couch there, if you put it under the mattress / it helps –

**JOE.** *Mom.*

**MAGGIE.** *(Turning to him.)* What, Joe?! What?!

**JOE.** Why can't I talk about this stuff?

**MAGGIE.** No one said you can't, I just think we can be done with it for the night!

**JOE**. Dr. Carl says it's healthy to talk about it, it makes me less anxious if / I'm able to –

**MAGGIE**. *(Losing herself a bit.)* Well she also says that you have the intelligence of a fifteen-year-old, so maybe you should listen to me when I –!

> *(Short pause.)*

For Christ's sake, let's just drop it.

> *(She resumes taking cushions off the couch. Silence.)*
>
> *(Then* **JOE** *suddenly slams both of his fists down on the coffee table, hard.)*

**BILLY**. / Okay, now –

**KEL**. Woah –

> *(***MAGGIE** *goes to* **JOE**.*)*

**MAGGIE**. Okay that's it, that's the line. I told you if it ever / got physical, that was the line –

**JOE**. Do you know how hard I've been trying since I've been back?! You're the one that came up to get me, you're the one that brought me back here!

**MAGGIE**. Calm down!

**JOE**. You have to stop making me feel like a freak!

**BILLY**. / Joe, let's just settle down –

**JOE**. She said I have the *social* intelligence of a fifteen-year-old! *Social* intelligence!

**MAGGIE**. Okay, fine, social intelligence! I'm wrong, you're right! But you have to calm down right now –

**JOE**. *Telling me to calm down doesn't help, it –...!*

> *(Short pause.)*

I'm going for a walk.

**MAGGIE**. Joe, I really don't think you should go walking around town this late –

**JOE**. When I get overwhelmed I can go for walks. We talked about this.

> *(He goes downstairs,* **MAGGIE** *follows him.)*

**MAGGIE.** I know we said that, but it's pitch black out there with all the streetlamps out, and Wayne might be / driving around –

**KEL.** I didn't mean to –

**BILLY.** / Kel, just –.

**JOE.** Let Wayne arrest me, I don't care!

**MAGGIE.** Joe I'm serious, he told us that he's not comfortable with you wandering around after dark!

**JOE.** Well let him shoot me, then! That'd be easier for everyone!

**MAGGIE.** Oh just / stop it –

**JOE.** You should have just left me in Anchorage, I don't know why you came to / get me –

**MAGGIE.** Can you *please* just go to your room to calm down? You can go for a walk in the morning, *please*!

> (**JOE** *storms out, slamming the door behind him.* **MAGGIE** *watches him go.*)
>
> (*Silence.* **MAGGIE** *takes a breath and heads back upstairs.*)

**KEL.** Are we still staying here?

**BILLY.** I don't know, Kel.

> (*Pause.*)

**KEL.** I'm sorry.

**BILLY.** Wasn't your fault.

> (**MAGGIE** *goes into the living room, heading toward the couch. She finishes pulling off all the cushions.*)

**MAGGIE.** Billy, grab that particle board from behind there, would you?

> (**BILLY** *pulls a large sheet of particle board from behind the couch.* **MAGGIE** *starts to pull the bed out of the couch.*)

**BILLY.** Oh here, Maggie, let me –

> (*He helps her pull the bed out.*)

**MAGGIE**. If either of you get hungry during the night, feel free to eat anything in the fridge there.

**BILLY**. Are you sure this is –?

**MAGGIE**. Fine, it's fine! He just needs to walk around a bit. He does this when he gets worked up, he just goes for walks, it calms him down.

**KEL**. I'm sorry if I –

**MAGGIE**. Oh honey, not your fault. He's just working through some stuff right now, that's all that it is.

> (**BILLY** *slides the particle board underneath the pull-out mattress.* **MAGGIE** *starts putting sheets on the bed.*)

**BILLY**. Oh, sure. I fly off the handle sometimes too, happens to everyone.

**MAGGIE**. Sure! We all just... Anyway.

**KEL**. When did he come back from Anchorage?

> (**MAGGIE** *continues putting the sheets on the bed.*)

**MAGGIE**. Oh, about four months ago now? Something like that?

**KEL**. What was he doing there?

**BILLY**. / Kel.

**MAGGIE**. Oh, I don't know, hon, I think he was mostly on the streets, he –...

> (*Pause.*)

> (**MAGGIE** *goes back to the bed, finishing with the sheets and pillows.*)

(*Looking at the bed.*) All right! Not too bad, right?

> (**MAGGIE** *and* **BILLY** *look at each other.*)

## Scene Four

> *(Later that night, outside, near the museum.* **JOE** *is sitting on the ground, alone, dimly lit by moonlight. On the second level,* **MAGGIE** *is asleep in her bedroom.* **BILLY** *is asleep on the pull-out.* **KEL** *is not in the space.)*

> *(After a moment,* **KEL** *enters, walking toward* **JOE. JOE** *sees her.)*

**KEL**. Hey.

**JOE**. Hi.

> *(Pause.)*

Your grandpa know you're out here?

**KEL**. No. He sleeps through everything, I just left.

> *(Pause.)*

Sorry if I made your mom upset at you.

**JOE**. It wasn't you, she was just –. I just needed to get outta there.

> *(**KEL** sits down with **JOE** on the ground.)*

**KEL**. You wanna smoke?

**JOE**. You have cigarettes? How old are you?

**KEL**. I'm fourteen. And no, I don't have cigarettes.

> *(She pulls out a one-hitter. Pause.)*

**JOE**. No, I –. Thanks.

**KEL**. You sure?

**JOE**. It's not a good idea.

**KEL**. Why? Would it make you see duck faces?

**JOE**. No. The stuff I was doing in Anchorage was a lot worse than pot.

> *(Pause.)*

You shouldn't smoke pot. You're too young.

**KEL**. How old were you when you first smoked pot?

**JOE**. Younger. But look how I turned out.

>(**KEL** *takes a hit off the one-hitter.* **JOE** *watches her. Pause.*)

**KEL**. I know you have problems or whatever, but at least you got out of town for a while, went to Anchorage. Most people don't even do that. As soon as I can, I'm getting out of Carmike Falls.

**JOE**. You might get out and then realize you had it a lot better back home.

**KEL**. Seriously, you don't know. Carmike Falls is really fucked up.

**JOE**. Everything seems fucked up when you're in high school. Nobody likes high school.

**KEL**. High school is *fine*. It's the rest of the town that's so fucked up.

**JOE**. How?

**KEL**. Well, for one, Minidoka was nearby.

**JOE**. I don't know what that is.

**KEL**. An internment camp.

>(*Short pause.*)

And like whenever I bring it up, people *freak out*. Not just the white people, Japanese too. Even my grandpa. And it's like – maybe I want to talk about this! Maybe we *should* talk about the fact that my great-grandma lived on a strawberry farm outside Seattle before her whole family was forced out by the government.

>(*Pause.*)

**JOE**. Wait, what?

**KEL**. When her family finally got out of Minidoka, their land had been stolen by the white farmer next door. So they took the closest farming jobs they could find. And I didn't even find this out from my family, I had to research this shit on my *own*.

>(*Pause.* **JOE** *stands up, wandering a bit.*)

**JOE.** That can't –... That can't be true.

**KEL.** You know that highway that connects Orofino and Missoula?

**JOE.** Yeah?

**KEL.** Built by Japanese-American prisoners.

*(Short pause. **JOE** thinks.)*

**JOE.** That just – really doesn't feel like it's true.

*(**KEL** chortles. Pause.)*

What are you guys doing up in Moscow again?

**KEL.** Mock legislature.

**JOE.** Oh, yeah. I did that. It was okay.

**KEL.** Ugh.

**JOE.** You're going to *Moscow* to do it? Why aren't you going to Boise?

**KEL.** *I know.* At least we did it in the actual state capital last year. This year we're doing it at a fucking Best Western, it's so dumb.

**JOE.** You have a bill or whatever?

**KEL.** Yep. I'm introducing a bill to make May 10th an official holiday in the state of Idaho. Carmike Falls Day.

**JOE.** What happened on May 10th?

**KEL.** Nothing.

**JOE.** Huh.

*(**KEL** takes another small hit from the one-hitter.)*

**KEL.** I'm not doing the one I wanted to do. My original bill was diverting funds from the Idaho National Guard into public education, my teacher said it was a bad idea.

**JOE.** Yeah, well, that is a bad idea.

**KEL.** Idaho is forty-ninth out of fifty in state funding for public education.

**JOE.** Education won't matter if you're dead. You need an army.

**KEL.** *(Rolling her eyes.)* Anyway.

> *(Short pause.)*

I don't even know if I believe in government anyway. It's all so stupid.

**JOE.** Well you came to the right place. With the vote and everything.

**KEL.** What vote?

**JOE.** Clements voted last week to unincorporate as a town.

**KEL.** I don't know what that means.

**JOE.** Just means that we're not gonna be a town anymore. No city services. That's why all the streetlights are out. No more money to keep the mine shaft safe for tourists. So we're shutting down the museum, last day is Sunday.

> *(Pause.)*

We're losing our stoplight, too.

**KEL.** Why did they vote to do that?

**JOE.** It's just so stupid. Last ten years or so, these rich people from California have been moving up here, buying up some of the land to build summer houses and ranches, and –. Anyway, there was this argument between this one family of rich jerks and these locals... The California people got, like, angry that the neighbors next door – who live in a fucking *trailer* – had like trash and abandoned cars on their property. So they like donated some money to town councilmembers or something stupid, got some laws passed about keeping your property free of garbage. People in town went nuts, it became this whole big thing. So all these people who've been living here for decades, have families that go back here for like a hundred and fifty years, they all decided to dissolve the town so they can't regulate the stupid garbage on the stupid yards.

> *(Pause.)*

It's like – they're just burning it all to the ground, it's so stupid.

(**KEL** *looks around.*)

KEL. Huh, that's –.

*(Short pause.)*

But I mean – it's not like much of a town anyway. The museum is like the only thing that isn't boarded up around here.

JOE. The café is still there.

KEL. For now. How many people even live in this town now?

JOE. I mean, it's gotten smaller, it's –. But I mean, being a town – it still *means* something.

KEL. I don't know, maybe it doesn't. Mean anything.

*(Pause.)*

You're too hard on your mom, you know.

(**JOE** *turns to her.*)

JOE. What?

KEL. She's trying. You need to give her a break.

JOE. Yeah, well, I'm trying too.

KEL. You're also like – how old? Are you in your thirties?

JOE. I'm twenty-seven.

KEL. Still. Twenty-seven-year-olds should have their shit together. You're still living with her, that's not how it's supposed to work. So you should just be nicer to her.

*(Pause.* **JOE** *gets up.)*

JOE. I'm gonna go to bed. Don't wake up anyone when you come back in.

KEL. Hey, do you think you could take me down into the mine tomorrow?

*(Pause.)*

JOE. What?

KEL. You can still go down, right?

*(Short pause.)*

JOE. No, they –. They closed it –

**KEL**. I won't tell anyone.

**JOE**. I'm not taking you down there, my mom would flip out.

**KEL**. C'mon, I wanna see it! We could go all the way down, to the bottom. We could see where the fire started, where your grandpa died.

**JOE**. No, that's –. No one's been all the way down for years, I haven't been down there since I was like eighteen –

**KEL**. Exactly, so you really wanna see it again, right?

*(Pause.)*

C'mon, just take me. You wanna go too, I know you do.

**JOE**. It's not like –... I don't know why you want to go down there, it's not like the mine is *haunted* or anything, it –

**KEL**. I don't believe in ghosts. I just wanna see where it happened, where those people actually died.

**JOE**. Why?!

**KEL**. I like looking at things that other people don't want to look at.

*(Pause.)*

Please.

*(Pause. **JOE** thinks.)*

**JOE**. I don't know if...

*(Pause.)*

I don't know if we even still have the keys to the elevator that goes to the sixty-four-hundred level.

*(Pause.)*

Seriously, I'm not sure, I'll have to look tomorrow.

**KEL**. Okay. I trust you.

*(Pause.)*

I'll see you tomorrow. I promise I won't make noise when I go inside.

*(Pause.)*

*(**KEL** exits back to the house. **JOE** watches her go.)*

## Scene Five

*(The next morning.)*

*(KEL is upstairs, asleep on the pull-out couch. BILLY is downstairs, barefoot, holding a cup of coffee. MAGGIE and JOE are not in the space.)*

*(BILLY is looking at the watch. He reaches up toward it, about to take it in his hand.)*

*(Just then, OLIVIA appears in the front windows, holding a tote bag. She looks inside, seeing BILLY. She goes to the front door, knocking on it. BILLY looks. OLIVIA motions for him to unlock the front door. BILLY goes to the door, unlocking and opening it.)*

BILLY. Hello?

OLIVIA. Hi there! Maggie's not around?

BILLY. Oh, I think she's still getting ready? Think I heard her head into the bathroom a bit ago.

> *(OLIVIA comes inside. BILLY, a bit confused, shuts the door behind her. OLIVIA offers a hand.)*

OLIVIA. I saw you here yesterday, I think! I'm Olivia.

BILLY. Oh – I'm an old friend of Maggie's, I'm / Billy –

OLIVIA. Billy Yamamoto! I know, I know it.

> *(She smiles at BILLY. Pause.)*

BILLY. Oh, sorry, have we [met] –?

OLIVIA. Nope, we've never met.

> *(Just then, MAGGIE emerges from the hallway upstairs, heading toward the stairs.)*

But I've heard a lot about you!

BILLY. Oh.

> *(Short pause.)*

O-kay then.

(**MAGGIE** *appears at the top of the stairs. She sees* **OLIVIA** *with* **BILLY**, *stops.*)

**OLIVIA.** Hi!

(*She smiles at* **BILLY**. **MAGGIE** *doesn't say anything. Finally, she moves toward* **BILLY** *and* **OLIVIA**.)

**MAGGIE.** (*To* **BILLY**.) That old pull-out bed do you and Kel okay?

**BILLY.** Oh, it was just fine.

**MAGGIE.** The bar in the middle give you any trouble?

**BILLY.** No, not at all. Slept just fine.

(**MAGGIE** *gives* **OLIVIA** *a look.*)

(**OLIVIA** *takes a clipboard out of her tote bag. She hands it to* **MAGGIE**.)

**OLIVIA.** Here, sign this.

**MAGGIE.** What is it?

**OLIVIA.** It's a petition, sign down there.

**MAGGIE.** Well what the heck am I signing?

**OLIVIA.** It's just saying that the results of the vote on 42 don't represent the best interests of the residents of Clements. Sign it.

(**MAGGIE** *moves away from* **OLIVIA**.)

**MAGGIE.** Oh, Livvy, I don't know what that means, I... Billy, you put coffee on?

**BILLY.** Right there, yep.

**OLIVIA.** Just sign it.

(**MAGGIE** *takes the petition, signing it.*)

**MAGGIE.** I'll sign the thing, but I just –. After all this crap, you really want to get into this again? You want coffee?

**OLIVIA.** Already had mine.

(**MAGGIE** *moves to the coffee maker, pours herself some coffee.*)

*(Upstairs,* **KEL***'s cell phone starts to ring.* **KEL** *slowly starts to wake up.* **OLIVIA** *eyes* **BILLY***.)*

**OLIVIA.** *(To* **BILLY***.)* So! You're just here for a visit?

(**MAGGIE** *glares at* **OLIVIA**. **KEL** *looks at her phone, momentarily unsure, then answers it tentatively, talking softly, heading downstairs.)*

**BILLY.** Just passing through, we stopped for the weekend. My granddaughter, she's got mock legislature down in Moscow on Monday.

*(Short pause.)*

I went to high school with Maggie.

**OLIVIA.** Oh, sure, I know.

*(Short pause.)*

So you're from Carmike Falls!

**BILLY.** That's right.

**OLIVIA.** And you two – went together for a time, right?

**MAGGIE.** Jesus, Livvy.

(**KEL** *appears at the top of the stairs.)*

**KEL.** *(Calling down.)* Grandpa.

**BILLY.** Yeah, honey?

**KEL.** Dad's on the phone.

**BILLY.** Okay, tell him I can call him back.

**KEL.** Grandpa, he doesn't sound good, you really should –...

*(Pause.* **BILLY** *nods at* **OLIVIA***, then heads upstairs.* **OLIVIA** *watches him go.)*

**BILLY.** *(On the phone.)* Patrick?

(**OLIVIA** *looks at* **MAGGIE***.)*

**MAGGIE.** What the hell is the matter with you?

**OLIVIA.** Well what's going on?!

**MAGGIE.** What, are you in the seventh grade? He's just passing through!

**OLIVIA.** Uh-huh.

**MAGGIE.** He told you, he's taking his granddaughter up to Moscow, so he –

**OLIVIA.** So he just decided to take a 120-mile detour over to Clements?!

> *(Upstairs,* **BILLY** *disappears down the hallway with the phone.)*

> *(***MAGGIE** *looks at* **OLIVIA.** *Pause.)*

**MAGGIE.** He's sick, Livvy.

> *(Pause.* **OLIVIA'S** *grin drops.)*

**OLIVIA.** Oh – I'm sorry, I didn't [realize] –...

> *(Pause.)*

How sick?

**MAGGIE.** It doesn't sound that bad yet, but still – life is short, and...

> *(Pause.)*

I guess he sold the farm a while back, bought a little place in town. He's asking me to go down there, with him. For good. And I don't know, I mean – it sounds crazy, but...

> *(Pause.* **OLIVIA** *thinks.)*

**OLIVIA.** Oh.

> *(***MAGGIE** *looks at her.)*

**MAGGIE.** What?

**OLIVIA.** Nothing, it's –

> *(The office door opens and* **JOE** *appears, coming up behind* **OLIVIA.**)*

**JOE.** Mom –

> *(***OLIVIA** *lets out a little shriek like before.)*

**OLIVIA.** Dammit, Joe, you need to stop doing that to me!

**JOE.** Oh, sorry.

> *(***JOE** *and* **MAGGIE** *look at one another. Pause.)*

**MAGGIE.** Didn't hear you wake up.

**JOE.** I got up early to do some work.

>*(Short pause.)*

**MAGGIE.** That's the last time you try something like that,
you hear me? I was up half the night waiting for you –

**JOE.** I'm sorry. I'm really grateful for you, and I'm sorry.

>*(**MAGGIE** looks away. Pause.)*

I was in the basement going through the old drill bits,
the ones you want to put on eBay? And I don't know
if –

**MAGGIE.** If you have a computer question, I won't be able
to help you, you'll just have to figure / it out yourself.

**JOE.** I feel like some of them aren't worth trying to sell.
Probably wouldn't get more than a few dollars for
them. I was wondering if you could tell me which ones
you think might make some money.

>*(**MAGGIE** looks at **JOE**. She takes a breath, then
>turns to **OLIVIA**.)*

**MAGGIE.** Gimme a few minutes?

**OLIVIA.** Oh, sure. I should be heading out anyway.

**MAGGIE.** Okay, then.

>*(**BILLY** comes back downstairs just as **MAGGIE**
>and **JOE** go into the office. He still has Kel's
>phone; he puts it in his pocket.)*

>*(Just as **OLIVIA** is about to go, she looks up
>and sees **BILLY**.)*

**OLIVIA.** Okay, I better get going.

**BILLY.** Okay, then.

>*(**OLIVIA** nearly leaves, but then turns back to
>**BILLY**.)*

**OLIVIA.** I know that you two – were together.

>*(Short pause.)*

**BILLY.** Well yeah, back in high school, we dated for a / bit –

**OLIVIA**. Not in high school. Fifteen or so years ago? When Caleb was still around?

(*Pause.* **BILLY** *doesn't know what to say.*)

I can't believe she managed to make it through that time. She was running this place all by herself, Caleb was no help, and Joe was *not* in a good place, he –... And there was that weekend when she told Caleb and Joe that she was going to Boise to see her aunt. But we're very close, you know. I knew something was going on. And she finally told me that she had gone to the Oregon coast, with you.

(*Pause.* **BILLY** *tenses up.*)

**BILLY**. Things between me and my wife... They weren't good.

**OLIVIA**. Sure, I get it. Things weren't good between her and Caleb either, that's for sure!

(*Pause.*)

She came back from that trip – I'd never seen her like that. She told me about driving around to all those little shore towns with you, staying in that bed and breakfast –

**BILLY**. We were –... We were both married.

**OLIVIA**. Yeah?

**BILLY**. We never did anything. We were both married, we stayed in separate rooms. We were faithful.

(*Pause.*)

**OLIVIA**. Maggie said you were sick, she didn't say what.

(**BILLY** *looks at her.*)

**BILLY**. It's –... Prostate cancer. Had it back in my forties, it came back.

(*Pause.*)

**OLIVIA**. Oh.

**BILLY**. But I beat it once, and I –

**OLIVIA**. Listen, I'm – *really* sorry to hear you're sick. I am. And please know I'm not trying to be cold, but...

(*Pause.*)

**OLIVIA.** I'm just saying – Maggie's spent most of her life taking care of men. Caleb, Joe… And her dad, he was no picnic, you know. She told me all about it, how he gave her such a hard time when you guys were dating.

(*Pause.* **BILLY** *looks at her.*)

You must have realized that, right? I mean – he was a World War II vet. Pacific Theater. And at a certain point I think he just put his foot down, he –… Anyway.

(*Pause, deliberate:*)

I'm sorry that you're sick. I really am. But – you get what I'm saying. Right?

(*Silence.* **BILLY** *looks at her.*)

(**KEL** *comes downstairs, going to* **BILLY**.)

Okay! I gotta go, it's gonna take me forever to get to all the farms on the edge of the county.

(*She exits. Pause.*)

**KEL.** Is Dad okay?

(*No response.*)

Grandpa?

**BILLY.** Yeah, he's –. He's fine, honey.

**KEL.** Are you sure?

**JOE.** (*Offstage.*) Shit.

**MAGGIE.** (*Offstage.*) Joe, what did you do that for?!

(**KEL** *and* **BILLY** *look.* **MAGGIE** *comes out of the office.*)

C'mon, over here –

(**JOE** *comes out as well, clutching his palm.*)

**KEL.** What happened?

**MAGGIE.** He cut himself on one of those diamond drill bits –

**JOE.** I really cut myself, it feels really deep –

**MAGGIE.** Over here.

*(She directs* **JOE** *over near the cash register. She finds some paper towels.)*

**BILLY**. He okay?

*(***MAGGIE*** tears off some paper towels, going to* **JOE**. *She looks at the wound, seeing a good amount of blood.)*

**MAGGIE**. He's fine, he...
*(Looking.)* Joe, you really did a number on yourself!

**JOE**. It's really bleeding –

**MAGGIE**. You might need some stitches. I think we're gonna have to go to that urgent care in Kellogg.

*(***BILLY*** gets up, going to them.)*

**BILLY**. Here, I can drive him –

**MAGGIE**. No, it's fine –

*(She starts ushering* **JOE** *outside.)*

**BILLY**. Really, Maggie, I'm happy to –

**MAGGIE**. *I'll take care of him.*

*(Short pause.)*

Thank you, I'll take care of it. Just keep the door locked, would you?

*(She flips the sign from "open" to "closed" as she and* **JOE** *exit.* **BILLY** *watches them go. He moves to the front door, locking it.)*

*(Silence.)*

**KEL**. Grandpa, are you sure Dad is okay? He sounded really bad.

**BILLY**. I gave Monty a call. He's on his way over right now to check on him. He'll be fine.

*(Pause.)*

**KEL**. Grandpa, maybe –... Maybe we should just go home.

*(***BILLY*** looks at* **KEL**.*)*

# ACT TWO

## Scene One

*(Afternoon.* **WAYNE**, *the county sheriff, sits on a chair on the ground floor eating a slice of cherry pie.* **MAGGIE** *sits with him.* **JOE** *is tinkering with a small exhibit in a corner, a wooden box with a large green button underneath some diagrams of a silver vein in the mine. He has a bandage around his palm.)*

**WAYNE.** And I pull him over, and I swear to you, the man looked like he had drank two bottles of vodka, easy. He had that glazed-over look, you know, like he was about to pass out right there. And I said, "Sir, do you know why I pulled you over? Any idea why I would have pulled you over today?" And he looks up at me and says something like –, I don't even know what he was trying to say, it was like – "Wuzza sped?"

**MAGGIE.** *(Laughing.)* Oh, God –

> (**WAYNE** *eats the pie, talking with his mouth full.)*

**WAYNE.** So I ask him to get out of the car, and he's falling all over himself, but I think he sorta got this spurt of energy when he got out of the car, and he – God, Maggie, this pie is amazing, you make this pie?

**MAGGIE.** Not the crust.

**WAYNE.** God, it's good. Anyway, I ask him to get out of the car and I think the blood sorta rushes to his brain – what's left of it – and he can sorta talk now, and he asks me why I pulled him over. And so I tell him that he was swerving – and he really was swerving a little – and that I seen him pull out of the 13 Club so I figured he'd had a drink or two, and he starts insisting that all he had was two beers. And I told him, well if that's true then you don't have anything to worry about!

**MAGGIE.** Two beers, / seems like he'd –

**WAYNE.** So I have him do the sobriety test, I did the thing where you hold up a pen and move it like this –

>   (*Moving his fingers horizontally.*)

– and I check out their eye movement to see if it's jerky, / or if it's –

**MAGGIE.** Is that what that test / is about?

**WAYNE.** No but wait for it. And I watch him and lo and behold – he follows it fine. No weird eye movements, totally normal. So then I do the thing where I ask him to walk in a straight line for nine steps then turn on one foot and –

>   (*Suddenly,* **MAGGIE'S VOICE** *is heard emanating from the small exhibit* **JOE***'s working on in the corner, loud.*)

**MAGGIE'S VOICE.** – Who discovered the now-famous Alexander vein in 1926, whose silver deposits were –

>   (**JOE** *manages to stop the recording.* **MAGGIE** *and* **WAYNE** *look at him. Pause.*)

**JOE.** Sorry.

**WAYNE.** *Anyway*, I have him do the thing where he has to walk the straight line, turn around and come back, and he does it, he doesn't miss a *single step*. Doesn't sway at all, walks a perfect line, all that. So then I'm thinking – well this guy can hold his liquor real well, can't he! So then I do the third test, and this is one that always gets 'em, where they have to stand on one foot and count to thirty, like – one one-thousand, two one-thousand, you know, without wobbling, / and so he –

**MAGGIE.** Thirty seems like / a lot –

**WAYNE**. No but wait for it. So he starts counting, and he – do you have any coffee?

**MAGGIE**. Oh, sure.

> *(She goes toward the coffee maker, pours* **WAYNE** *a cup as he talks.)*

**WAYNE**. And so he starts counting and I'm like, by god he's actually doing it, he's on one leg and he's not wobbling at all –

> *(**MAGGIE'S VOICE** starts again, even louder.)*

**MAGGIE'S VOICE**. – Alexander vein in 1926, whose –

> *(**JOE** stops the recording.)*

**JOE**. Sorry.

**MAGGIE**. Joe, just leave it alone for / God's sake.

**JOE**. I've almost fixed it.

**MAGGIE**. *(To* **WAYNE**.*)* You want cream or sugar?

**WAYNE**. No, no, thank you. *Anyway* so he gets up to thirty and I just let him keep going, I let him get all the way to sixty before I stopped him. I couldn't believe it.

**MAGGIE**. I don't even know / if I could –

**WAYNE**. No but wait for it! So then he looks at me all proud, you know, like this proud idiot, and he says to me – "You couldn't arrest me anyway!" And I had no idea what the hell he was talking about, so I said, "Excuse me?" And he said, "I just voted to dissolve this town, and we won! So I don't have to obey your laws anymore!"

> *(**MAGGIE** brings him his coffee.)*

**MAGGIE**. *(Laughing.)* Lord, my lord.

**WAYNE**. So then I have to explain to this joker – just because Clements isn't a town anymore, that doesn't mean it's a free-for-all. There are still *laws*. Like, he thought he was suddenly living in the Wild West or something!

**MAGGIE**. Who was this guy again?

**WAYNE.** Oh, I shouldn't say his name. You'd recognize him, one of those old out-of-work miners, that group of guys that're at the 13 Club all day long. You'd recognize him.

**MAGGIE.** Hank?

**WAYNE.** Nah, not Hank, Hank's a good guy. I really shouldn't say.

**MAGGIE.** Well that's just –. So you had to let him go?

**WAYNE.** Oh, no, I gave him the breathalyzer. Point five one. Surprised he wasn't dead.

*(He takes another bite of pie. Pause.)*

**MAGGIE.** It's just gonna be a little weird around here for a while, I think. People are just gonna get weird for a bit.

**WAYNE.** People'll calm down. Just give it some time.

*(Pause.)*

**MAGGIE.** *(Re: the pie.)* You want another piece?

**WAYNE.** Oh no, I'd pass out behind the wheel.

**MAGGIE.** Well. Thanks so much for taking us to the urgent care like that.

*(Re:* **JOE.***)* Butter fingers over here.

**WAYNE.** Glad I was passing by as you guys were leaving.

**MAGGIE.** I've never been in the back of a police car before, that was fun! Those things go fast. Wasn't that fun, Joe?

**JOE.** Mm-hm.

**MAGGIE.** They gonna give you a different car now?

**WAYNE.** No, same one. Just gonna change the decal on the side, starting next month it'll say "sheriff."

**MAGGIE.** Well that's so exciting for you, it really is. I'm so glad you got elected.

**WAYNE.** One good thing to come out of this whole mess.

**MAGGIE.** I felt so proud when I saw your name on that ballot.

*(A lull in the conversation. Finally:)*

**WAYNE.** You know what actually I might have just a tiny bit more of that pie?

**MAGGIE.** Oh, sure!

*(**WAYNE** starts to get up.)*

**WAYNE.** Is it just up in the kitchen, or –?

**MAGGIE.** No, no! You stay here, I'll be right back.

> *(She grabs the plate and heads upstairs.)*
>
> *(Pause. **JOE** continues to tinker with the exhibit.)*
>
> *(**WAYNE** gets up, walking over to **JOE**. Upstairs, **MAGGIE** goes into the kitchen.)*

**WAYNE.** How's the hand?

**JOE.** Hurts.

**WAYNE.** Yeah, well, you sliced it real good. How many stitches?

**JOE.** Five.

**WAYNE.** Nice.

> *(Pause.)*

So must be good being back in town, huh?

> *(**JOE** looks at him.)*

**JOE.** …Yeah.

**WAYNE.** How long has it been? Four, five years?

**JOE.** More like six, I think.

**WAYNE.** Right, right, six years ago… So you were about twenty-one and Olivia's kid was around twelve or so when you attacked him. That makes sense.

> *(He starts wandering around the space, looking at photos, maps, etc. **JOE** watches him.)*

**JOE.** I didn't –… I didn't *attack* him –

**WAYNE.** Oh, sure. I guess you're right, no charges filed, Livvy and Bill had mercy, it's a good thing.

> *(Pause. **JOE** looks at him.)*

**JOE.** I have a psychiatrist now.

**WAYNE.** That's good, I'm glad to hear it.

**JOE.** And I'm taking medication, it helps with the –. I really am getting better, Wayne –

**WAYNE.** I hear you, I do. And that's great you're getting better.

    *(Pause.)*

I've known your mom for a long time, Joe. I care deeply about her well-being.

    **(MAGGIE** *comes back down the stairs with* **WAYNE**'s *plate.)*

**MAGGIE.** I remembered we had some ice cream, I put a scoop on there for you.

**WAYNE.** Oh you didn't need to do that –

**MAGGIE.** It's just vanilla.

    *(She hands* **WAYNE** *the plate. He sits back down, taking a bite.)*

**WAYNE.** So now that the place is shutting down, what are you gonna be up to?

**MAGGIE.** Oh, you know. Retirement, I guess. I've held off on the social security checks, but I suppose I can start letting those come in. I don't need much. Guess I'll just sit around here and get old. Older.

**WAYNE.** Aw, c'mon.

**MAGGIE.** I don't mind it, I don't mind being an old lady. People are nice to you, they don't expect you to do anything. I was at the car wash the other day, the manual one in Kellogg? And this young guy who was washing his car next to me *insisted* on doing it for me. I just had to sit back and watch him, it was full service!

**WAYNE.** Well then!

**MAGGIE.** I said to him, I don't mind looking like some old lady if people wait on me like that. Fine by me.

**WAYNE.** Well I don't think you look a day over forty.

**MAGGIE.** C'mon.

**WAYNE.** I'm serious! You look just like you did when you were giving those mine tours when you were in your twenties.

    *(MAGGIE blushes. JOE rolls his eyes.)*

**MAGGIE.** Oh, stop it.

**WAYNE**. I'm serious! I still remember when I was a kid, going on those mine tours – God did I have a crush on you.

**MAGGIE**. You did not!

**WAYNE**. Hand to God.

**MAGGIE**. I can't believe I've known you that long. And now look at you, county sheriff.

**WAYNE**. Oh it's nothing big.

**MAGGIE**. Nothing big my foot! You got elected, that's a big deal.

**JOE**. Who did you run against?

>    *(Pause.* **WAYNE** *and* **MAGGIE** *look at* **JOE**. **MAGGIE** *gives* **JOE** *a look.)*

**WAYNE**. I ran unopposed.

**JOE**. Oh, right.

>    *(Pause.)*

But still, yeah, it's a big deal I guess.

**MAGGIE**. Joe.

>    *(A tense pause.* **WAYNE** *stares at* **JOE**. *Finally,* **WAYNE***'s radio starts squawking.)*

**WAYNE**. Ugh.

>    *(He talks into his radio:)*

Copy. Go ahead, Ellen.

>    *(He excuses himself wordlessly, heading to a corner of the room. He listens to his radio.)*

>    *(***MAGGIE*** goes to* **JOE**.*)*

**MAGGIE**. *(Whispering.)* What the hell was that?!

**JOE**. *(Whispering.)* I don't like him.

**WAYNE**. *(Into the radio.)* Copy.

>    *(He turns back to* **MAGGIE**.*)*

I gotta go. This lady calls me once a week thinking someone stole her damn dog, it's –. Anyway, life of the public servant.

*(He gets up to go.)*

**MAGGIE.** Who is it?

**WAYNE.** I can't say.

*(Pause.)*

Tina Hudson.

**MAGGIE.** Oh yeah, she's nuts.

**WAYNE.** Yeah, well, I didn't say anything. Thanks for the pie.

**MAGGIE.** Well, thank you for the fancy ride in the cop car!

*(**WAYNE** heads toward the door. He claps **JOE**'s back on his way out, maybe a bit too hard. **JOE** winces.)*

*(**WAYNE** exits. **MAGGIE** goes to **JOE**.)*

You be respectful to him.

**JOE.** He's a jerk. He hates me for no reason, he always has.

**MAGGIE.** Oh he doesn't hate you.

**JOE.** Do you know how many times he stopped me when I was a teenager? When I'd just be walking home, or coming back from Dan's house? He'd pull up beside me and shine that spotlight in my face –

**MAGGIE.** Well were you doing anything?

**JOE.** No! I was just walking home!

**MAGGIE.** You were probably doing something.

*(**JOE** continues to mess with the exhibit. **MAGGIE** sits down near him, watching him tinker.)*

*(Silence.)*

Joe, when the doctor was looking at your hand, I noticed that scar on the other side, there. Where'd you get that thing?

*(**JOE** looks at the top of his hand.)*

**JOE.** Oh, it's –. I don't know.

**MAGGIE.** You don't *know*? How can you not know? The thing is huge.

*(Short pause.)*

**JOE.** I just don't know if you wanna hear about this stuff. Like, if you want to hear about the last few years. Maybe you'd be happier not knowing.

*(No response.)*

Guy slashed me with a hunting knife outside of a bar.

**MAGGIE.** Oh, God.

**JOE.** It wasn't that bad.

**MAGGIE.** He –?! Why'd he do that?!

**JOE.** I deserved it.

*(Short pause.)*

I was hanging around outside, and when he came out, I saw the duck face on him, and I got freaked out and –. Anyway.

**MAGGIE.** How long ago was that?

**JOE.** I don't know. Couple years? Three maybe?

*(Pause.)*

**MAGGIE.** Were you seeing those faces all the time, or –?

**JOE.** You said I should only talk to Dr. Carl about this stuff –

**MAGGIE.** Yeah, well. I'm asking you.

*(Pause.)*

**JOE.** There were phases. Some worse than others. When that guy cut me, it was bad. I was seeing them all the time. Almost everybody. Didn't feel safe anywhere.

*(Pause.)*

**MAGGIE.** But you haven't seen any since you've been back, right?

**JOE.** No, Mom. I told you.

**MAGGIE.** Good, that's good.

*(She pauses, smiling at **JOE**.)*

*(Re: the exhibit.)* Just chuck that thing, it's worthless. I hate the sound of my own voice, anyway.

(**JOE** *rubs his eyes a bit.*)

**MAGGIE.** You okay?

**JOE.** Yeah, it's just –. Painkillers they gave me are making me feel weird.

**MAGGIE.** You could nap for a while before Billy and Kel get back?

**JOE.** Okay.

> (*He starts to head upstairs. He stops, turning back to* **MAGGIE.**)

Why did you come get me?

**MAGGIE.** What?

**JOE.** Why did you come up to Alaska, why did you bring me back here?

> (*Pause.*)

**MAGGIE.** Joe, I –. I don't know what you mean –

**JOE.** I mean when I finally went up to Alaska, it must have been a relief for you –

**MAGGIE.** A *"relief"*?

**JOE.** Yeah, I mean, it must have been really awful for you when I was here. It was bad enough that your husband was gay, left you to move in with some random guy he met on the internet, and now you have this kid who's wandering around town refusing to talk to anybody –

**MAGGIE.** / Okay –

**JOE.** So it was probably *nice* for you when I finally left town –

**MAGGIE.** *Okay*, Joe!

**JOE.** Just say that I embarrassed you! Say that maybe it was nice that I left for a while!

> (*Pause.*)

It's okay!

> (*Pause.*)

**MAGGIE.** Joe, you put me through *hell* when you up and left like that. You understand me?

**JOE**. So why did you let me go?

**MAGGIE**. I didn't have a choice! You were a twenty-one-year old man, what was I supposed to do? After what happened with Cam, there were plenty of people who wanted me to call the psych ward over at Kootenai Memorial. You know that, right?

**JOE**. That wouldn't have helped.

**MAGGIE**. I know it! But that was my only other option, having you locked up somewhere. Believe me, when you announced to me that you were moving up there – your dad told me, "Just let him go, maybe it'll be good for him." Part of me wanted to throw myself in front of that bus rather than have you thousands of miles away.

> *(Pause.)*

I'm not sure what story you've been telling yourself these last few months, but when you stopped calling me like normal, when I didn't know if you were even *alive* – I spent nine hundred dollars to fly up to Anchorage, find you, and bring you back here. Nine hundred dollars that I *didn't have*. And if you left again tomorrow and stopped calling me, I'd do the same goddam thing again.

> *(Pause. **JOE** takes a few steps toward **MAGGIE**. **MAGGIE** goes to him and they hug one another.)*
>
> *(Silence.)*

You're back. You're *back* now, you hear me? And you can't leave again. You can't do that to me again, I couldn't take it.

> *(Pause.)*

You smell bad, why do you smell so bad?

**JOE**. Sorry.

**MAGGIE**. Just wondering why you smell so bad.

**JOE**. I should shower.

**MAGGIE**. Yeah, you should.

(*JOE breaks the hug. He looks at* **MAGGIE**. *Pause.*)

**MAGGIE**. We could get out of here, you know.

(*Short pause.*)

I'm just saying, we don't need to stay here, once we get this place all closed up. Might be too many bad memories around here.

**JOE**. Where'd we go?

**MAGGIE**. I don't know, just –. This town isn't – or whatever it is now, this *place*... There's nothing here for us now.

(*Pause.*)

I don't know. Something to think about.

(*Pause.*)

**JOE**. I should shower.

(*He heads upstairs.* **MAGGIE** *watches him go.*)

## Scene Two

*(Outside, shortly later.* **KEL** *is sitting on the ground, typing on her phone. Upstairs the only person visible in the house is* **BILLY**, *sitting on the pull-out couch in the living room, lost in thought.)*

*(***KEL**'s *phone starts ringing. She sees who it is. She immediately tenses up, doesn't know what to do. She stands up.)*

*(She almost lets the call go to voicemail, but then answers it. She brings the phone to her ear.)*

**KEL**. You're not supposed to be calling me.

*(She takes a breath, listening, becoming a bit more comfortable.)*

I know, Dad, I –. Yeah, I'm –. I'm fine. You know Grandpa, he's nice but he like barely talks in the car. There's just like these really long silences and then finally he'll say something awkward like, "So Mock Legislature, huh?"

*(Pause.)*

Yeah.

*(***JOE** *enters, watching* **KEL**. **KEL** *doesn't notice.)*

*(Pause.* **KEL** *listens for a moment, taking a breath, becoming a little upset.)*

I miss you, too.

*(Pause.)*

No, Dad, I –... Because it's too hard being around you when you're –... Of course I want to come back home, but it's not about that, it... Dad, stop. Please, Dad –.

*(Pause.* **JOE** *takes a step toward* **KEL**.*)*

You know, if you have to drink, maybe you could just drink beer? Maybe you could just drink the beer that's in the garage, you –...

*(Just then, she sees* **JOE.***)*

**KEL.** I have to go.

*(She hangs up.)*

*(Pause.)*

**JOE.** Hey.

(**KEL** *turns around, putting the phone in her pocket, gathering herself.)*

You okay?

**KEL.** I'm fine. How's your hand?

**JOE.** It hurts but it's okay.

*(Pause.)*

Who were you talking to?

**KEL.** Were you listening to me?

**JOE.** I was just waiting until you were done.

*(Pause.)*

**KEL.** Did you get the keys?

*(Pause.)*

**JOE.** We really shouldn't do this.

**KEL.** We'll be quick.

**JOE.** What about your grandpa?

**KEL.** I told him I'm just wandering around town. He's fine, he gives me space.

*(Pause.)*

**JOE.** You know, I had a hard time with my dad, too.

**KEL.** What?

**JOE.** I'm just saying, I get it. My dad never listened to me either, I never knew how to talk to him or –

**KEL.** I'm not like you.

*(Pause.)*

You ready?

*(Pause.* **KEL** *exits.* **JOE** *follows her.)*

## Scene Three

> *(Early evening.* **BILLY** *and* **MAGGIE** *are alone together downstairs, a few beers deep. They're having a good time.)*

**MAGGIE.** What was that kid's name?

**BILLY.** Oh, I don't – was it Charlie?

**MAGGIE.** No, you're thinking of Charlie Baxter.

**BILLY.** Oh, that's right, / Charlie Baxter –

**MAGGIE.** Anyway he was so mad that you ended up taking me to prom, he was about ready to run you over with that Nash Rambler of his, that big red thing –

**BILLY.** Those were good cars, I had / one of those later on.

**MAGGIE.** You remember how mad he got?

**BILLY.** Oh, I don't even remember the kid's name –

**MAGGIE.** I had no idea he even wanted to ask me out! Not like I was the belle of the ball or anything when I was a teenager –

**BILLY.** Oh you were okay.

> *(Short pause.* **MAGGIE** *looks at him.)*

**MAGGIE.** "Okay"?

**BILLY.** I meant to say –

**MAGGIE.** Oh I was "okay," well then!

**BILLY.** You were beautiful.

> *(Pause.)*

You were beautiful.

> *(Short pause.)*

**MAGGIE.** Anyway, he ended up taking that girl who was kind of big, the bigger girl. Maxine? The bigger girl.

**BILLY.** Oh sure.

**MAGGIE.** I mean not that big.

**BILLY.** Sure, / not that big.

**MAGGIE.** But he came up to me at the dance – do you remember this?

**BILLY.** No, I don't / think so –

**MAGGIE.** He marched right up to me at that dance, and he just sort of *declared* to me, "I'm here with Maxine." And poor Maxine, God knows what she was thinking, she must have been so embarrassed. But I was oblivious, I had no idea he wanted to take me in the first place, so here's poor Maxine –

**BILLY.** *(Re: beer.)* You want another?

**MAGGIE.** Sure.

> (**BILLY** *heads into the office for another beer.*)

And I look at him, and I said "that's nice" because I had no idea what the heck was even going on –

**BILLY.** *(Offstage, calling out.)* Tom!

**MAGGIE.** What's that?

> (**BILLY** *re-enters with a couple of fresh cans of beer.*)

**BILLY.** Tom! Tom Anderson, / that was his name.

**MAGGIE.** Tom! That's right, Tom Anderson! So anyway I guess Tom was pretty mad at you.

**BILLY.** Yep, I'm remembering now, it's coming back to me now.

**MAGGIE.** It is?

**BILLY.** Yep. He had some words for me.

**MAGGIE.** Oh, I bet he did.

**BILLY.** Up until this moment I had no idea why the guy was so mad at me.

**MAGGIE.** Well, now you know, you stole me away from him!

**BILLY.** He called me a "pan face." In front of all the other guys, in the locker room during Phys Ed. Right around that time, I think.

> *(Pause.* **MAGGIE** *is shocked.)*

**MAGGIE.** He did not.

**BILLY.** Oh, sure. I remember that, clear as day.

**MAGGIE.** He really called you that?!

**BILLY.** At the time I thought it was because I knocked him too hard when we were playing basketball, something / like that –

**MAGGIE.** I can't believe he said that!

**BILLY.** Oh, you know. He was from a poorer family. Not too bright, either.

**MAGGIE.** I just still can't believe it.

(Pause.)

Did you hear that from other people growing up?

**BILLY.** Oh, you know. Not so bad.

(Pause. They drink.)

After your family moved back up here, I got this job down at the grocery store, you remember that little grocery store that guy Nils used to run?

**MAGGIE.** Oh, sure, the Swedish family. They sold that disgusting fish thing, that fish thing that was like jelly.

**BILLY.** Lutefisk.

**MAGGIE.** Boy, that was disgusting.

**BILLY.** I thought it was all right.

**MAGGIE.** I never tried it. Ech.

**BILLY.** Nils had that brother Erik, he was a vet. Stationed in Papua New Guinea during the war. My dad came over to pick me up one time, I was getting my stuff together in the back and I heard this scuffle, something going on, my dad shouting. It was so crazy, my dad never raised his voice. So I come out, and there's Erik and my dad, just about ready to tear each other apart.

**MAGGIE.** What happened?

**BILLY.** That's the thing, it was some stupid disagreement, something about my dad's car outside not being parked right. But man, did they get into it. Erik starts screaming in my dad's face, all these insults, words I'd never even *heard*. Screaming that him and his family should get put back into the camps, that he... Some customer called the police, they came over. Cop grabbed my dad, shoved him in the back of his cop car. He almost spent the night in jail. I tried to talk to him about it the next day, he wouldn't say a word.

    *(Pause.)*

Sorry, I don't know where I was going with that one, why was I telling that story?

**MAGGIE.** Oh, I'm not / sure –

**BILLY.** I'm like Henry Fonda in that movie.

**MAGGIE.** What's that?

**BILLY.** Oh you, the – pond, the –. Skip it. I'm getting old.

    *(Pause.)*

**MAGGIE.** But Carmike Falls was a good place to grow up, right?

**BILLY.** Oh, sure. Lots of nice people.

**MAGGIE.** And the fiddling festival. That's really nice.

**BILLY.** Oh, sure.

    *(Pause. **BILLY** takes a drink. He looks at **MAGGIE**.)*

Maggie, you know...

**MAGGIE.** Hm?

**BILLY.** I just want to make certain you know... I'm not inviting you down to Carmike Falls to be my nurse or anything. I've dealt with this cancer thing before, I can handle it myself, I'm not gonna be some invalid or / something –

**MAGGIE.** Billy, what are / you –?

**BILLY.** I just don't want you thinking that I'm only here because I need someone to take care of me when I'm sick, / I'm not –

**MAGGIE.** That never even occurred to me, I'm not...

    *(Short pause, thinking.)*

Did Livvy say something to you?

**BILLY.** Oh, no –

**MAGGIE.** *(Realizing.)* She said something to you.

**BILLY**. She's just concerned for you, she's being a good friend.

**MAGGIE**. That dumb hen, what did she say?

**BILLY**. She just wants to make sure some sick guy isn't swooping into town and forcing you to / move your whole –

**MAGGIE**. You're not forcing / me to –

**BILLY**. And I want you to know that – of course – this is up to you. If you felt like moving down there for a bit, you –. But I want to be respectful, I haven't been in your life for quite some time, and Olivia obviously knows you real well –

**MAGGIE**. Trust me, what Olivia doesn't know could fill that mine out there, I promise you.

*(Pause.)*

Whatever I do, Billy, it's for me, not for you. I move down there with you, it's because I want to. Me.

*(Pause.)*

**BILLY**. You know, Livvy also...

**MAGGIE**. Oh God, what else did she say?

**BILLY**. I don't want to get her in trouble.

**MAGGIE**. Too late. What?

*(Pause.)*

**BILLY**. Back when we were first dating, when you broke it off with me... Did your dad tell you to do it?

*(Pause.)*

**MAGGIE**. You know my dad was in the war –

**BILLY**. Sure –

**MAGGIE**. Pacific Theater –

**BILLY**. I know it.

**MAGGIE**. And he was so good about us at first. He knew that we were going together. He even drove me a few times to meet you at the movie theater, never said a word. And he was polite to you, right? He was always polite?

**BILLY**. Sure, he was great.

**MAGGIE**. But, you know, this stuff runs deep, and he... There came a point where he just told me I – couldn't be with you.

**BILLY**. And you listened to him.

(*Short pause.*)

**MAGGIE**. I know I could have refused to go with him, I could have stayed in Carmike Falls. I was almost eighteen, after all. But you gotta understand, my dad – he wasn't doing so well around then, and I didn't think I could just abandon him. When he decided to move us back to Clements, I thought maybe the change would do him good, but he just got worse, and –...

(*Pause.*)

He used to see things down in the mine, when he was working alone. Kids wandering around the tunnels in the dark, screaming for help, all kinds of... It's probably where Joe gets it. I'd go to my mom, tell her that we needed to get him help, she wouldn't listen to me, she... After a while it felt like I was the only one taking care of him.

(*Pause.* **MAGGIE** *looks down.*)

**BILLY**. What finally made him put his foot down about us, move you all back up to Clements?

(*Pause.*)

**MAGGIE**. That night, after prom – when we went up to the water tower park?

**BILLY**. I remember.

**MAGGIE**. When we made that decision, up there, I thought –... I know we were just kids, not even eighteen yet. But you know, I was so excited, thinking we might get married. It was like I could see my whole life in front of me that night, and it looked so – nice, it...

(*Pause.*)

Anyway, the next day I was so excited I told my sister that we were planning on getting married, and of course she went and blabbed to my dad. And boy, did he have some words for me.

*(Pause. BILLY takes this in.)*

And of course that was so stupid of me to think that, we were only seventeen and we were just *talking*, you weren't ready to propose to me or / anything –

BILLY. I thought I'd proposed, Maggie. I thought I'd proposed, and I thought you'd said yes. Felt as real as anything to me. I was even planning on going out and buying a ring that week.

*(Pause.)*

Back then I thought maybe I'd make it to college, the U of I. Maybe even study medicine, go on to med school, something like that. And I thought maybe we could both go to college together, by the time we finished we could get married.

*(Pause.)*

But then you broke things off with me, your family moved back up here, and –. Taking over the farm from my dad just seemed a lot simpler.

*(Pause.)*

MAGGIE. God, and now we've gotten so old. How'd we get so old?

*(They sit with one another for a moment. Then, BILLY reaches over and takes MAGGIE's hand in his.)*

*(Silence.)*

BILLY. It could be good, you know.

MAGGIE. I know.

*(Pause.)*

Billy – you know I'd have to take Joe with me. I can't do this unless I can take him with me.

*(Short pause.)*

**BILLY.** I get it, Maggie.

**MAGGIE.** He's a handful.

**BILLY.** You know what? Joe's okay. Might even be good for him.

**MAGGIE.** *(Smiling.)* It might be.

> *(She looks at* **BILLY.***)*

> *(Just then,* **OLIVIA** *barges in through the front door.)*

Well, look who it is.

> *(She goes to* **OLIVIA.***)*

**OLIVIA.** We need to talk.

**MAGGIE.** Well good, I've got some words for you too.

**BILLY.** / Mags –

**OLIVIA.** What?

**MAGGIE.** What the hell did you say to Billy?

**BILLY.** Oh, I / didn't mean to –

**OLIVIA.** What? I didn't say anything to him –

**MAGGIE.** Really? Nothing about my dad, nothing about you not wanting me to go down to Carmike Falls?

> *(Pause.)*

**OLIVIA.** I wasn't –. I was just looking out for you –

**MAGGIE.** Well I can look out for myself, thank you very much. I don't know how many times I have to go through this with you! Last month when you told Fred Kingston that he overcharged me for replacing the engine in my car –

**OLIVIA.** You *told* me he overcharged you!

**MAGGIE.** Well I didn't need you going over there and screaming at him for me! Now I don't have any place around here where I can take my car!

**BILLY.** She really wasn't trying to –

**MAGGIE.** Don't you be nice to her about it, she's always doing this.

**OLIVIA.** Maggie.

**MAGGIE.** Every town has one, a fixer. The person who makes everyone else's business into *their* business just because they're too bored with their own –

**OLIVIA.** Did you vote yes on 42?

*(Pause. **MAGGIE** looks at her.)*

**MAGGIE.** What?

**OLIVIA.** Did you vote yes? Did you vote to unincorporate the town?

*(**MAGGIE** stops, unsure of how to respond. Pause.)*

I was out driving around to those farms on the edge of the county near Mullan, I showed the petition to this guy, and he sees your name on there and says that you told him last week you voted yes.

*(Pause.)*

**MAGGIE.** Okay, now –. Now who exactly is this?

**OLIVIA.** I don't remember his name –

**MAGGIE.** Well then how am I supposed to know what you're talking about?!

*(**OLIVIA**, flustered, takes the petition out of her tote bag. She looks at it for a moment, finding the name. **MAGGIE** busies herself with cleaning out the coffee maker, dumping the used grounds and filter into the trash.)*

*(**OLIVIA** finds the name.)*

**OLIVIA.** Alan Knowles, that's / his name.

**MAGGIE.** *Alan Knowles?* Oh, he doesn't know what the hell he's / talking about –

**OLIVIA.** He said that he came over last week to work on your upstairs bathroom, and that he talked with you about it all afternoon, and you told him you voted yes.

**MAGGIE.** Livvy, I am so sick of this talk, I really am –

**OLIVIA.** Why did you tell him that?

**MAGGIE.** Alan Knowles is just annoyed that I gave him grief over the job he did on that sink up there, which was / totally –

**OLIVIA.** *Maggie.*

> (**MAGGIE** *finally stops, looking at* **OLIVIA**. *Tense pause.*)
>
> (**BILLY** *moves to exit.*)

**BILLY.** I can [leave you two alone]...

**MAGGIE.** You don't need to go anywhere.

> (*Pause.*)

You know, Livvy, believe it or not – not everyone in this world agrees with everything that you think. I know that you'd like to believe that whatever is clanging around in that head of yours is the prevailing opinion of everyone you come into contact with, but believe it or not – other opinions exist!

> (**OLIVIA** *is at a loss.*)

**OLIVIA.** I just can't believe it. I really / can't, Maggie.

**MAGGIE.** Oh would you just stop it?

**OLIVIA.** You of all people?! You have so much history here, more than anyone I know! I just don't understand, I didn't know you were this dumb!

> (*Pause.* **MAGGIE** *stares at* **OLIVIA.**)

**MAGGIE.** Say that to me again.

**OLIVIA.** I didn't mean –

**MAGGIE.** I'm serious. Say that to me one more time.

> (*Pause.*)

I've known you all your life, Livvy. I was at your high school graduation. When your mom passed, I babysat you when your dad was too upset to be around you. But I'm not going to be friends with anyone who thinks that about me, who says that to my face.

> (*Pause.*)

**OLIVIA**. *You're being dumb, Maggie.*

> *(Pause.)*

Maybe I gave you too much credit, I guess I figured you had done the work, you had actually thought this decision through. And not just about the mine, I know that you didn't see that coming, no one did. But at the end of the day, someone put a piece of paper in front of you and asked you to make a decision. They asked you whether or not you think that your community mattered. It's not just about a stoplight, or funding to keep some old mine safe. They asked you a simple question: Do you want to keep your community together, or blow it apart? And you voted to blow it apart. And that was a *dumb* thing to do.

> *(Silence. **OLIVIA** seethes.)*

**MAGGIE**. Exactly what has this community done for me, Livvy?

**OLIVIA**. You're honestly asking me that question?

**MAGGIE**. I'm honestly asking you / that question.

**OLIVIA**. Well, I'd say that it's given your family employment for, what, over a hundred years now? And it's given you your livelihood, your *community*, we've all been there for you, *and* Joe –

**MAGGIE**. I remember my dad coming home every morning from his shifts out in Dodson. He only worked nights, when we moved back here, they only gave him night shifts, didn't matter that his dad, his granddad, had worked in that mine, spent their entire lives down there. He'd come home, covered in sweat from the heat down there, holding that two-gallon jug of water he'd go through every night.

> *(Pause.)*

Never one complaint. You'd ask him about his job, he'd be the first to tell you how much he appreciated having the work. He was fifty-two years old and they still had him on the night shift, paying him two dollars and twenty-six cents an hour, when that fire started and he got cooked like a goddam rotisserie chicken, a mile underneath that mountain. And what did the town do for us then? They put his name in the paper. Put a little plaque on the wall of the mine. My mother worked two jobs after that until the day she died.

(*Pause.*)

Up to me? I'd have that mine filled with garbage and sealed off *tomorrow*.

(*Pause.* **MAGGIE** *stares at* **OLIVIA**, **OLIVIA** *looks away.*)

**OLIVIA.** Maggie, I'm sorry, but you have to / realize –

**MAGGIE.** And now these people from California moving in here with their five-bedroom houses, with their SUVs they drive to the ski slopes on the weekends, with their little rich kids with their brand-new phones that I spend all day long taking down into that mine, and *they* tell us...

(*Short pause, deliberately:*)

They tell *us* – we aren't keeping our yards clean enough.

(*Silence.*)

(**OLIVIA** *has run out of steam. She sits down.*)

**OLIVIA.** I just...

(*Pause.*)

I just –. I don't understand anymore. I really don't.

(*She starts to become upset. She tears up.* **MAGGIE** *softens.*)

**MAGGIE.** Okay, just –.

(*Pause, stern:*)

Livvy, stop it. Stop crying please.

**OLIVIA.** I can't help it.

**MAGGIE.** Yes you can, just stop it!

**OLIVIA.** I can't help it!

**MAGGIE.** Oh for Christ's sake. Billy, run and get some toilet paper?

> (**BILLY** *goes to the office.* **MAGGIE** *goes to* **OLIVIA**, *rubbing her back.*)

You'll be fine. We're all gonna be fine.

**OLIVIA.** I really don't know, Maggie, I honestly don't. Everything's changing, the town's falling apart, you might be leaving for good –

**MAGGIE.** Is that what this is all about? You'll still see me.

**OLIVIA.** Carmike Falls is so far away!

**MAGGIE.** I'm not even sure I'm –... Livvy, if we go, it's not that far away.

**OLIVIA.** Seven-hour drive!

**MAGGIE.** Lord, is it really that far?

**OLIVIA.** Uh-huh!

**MAGGIE.** How do you know that?

**OLIVIA.** I looked it up on my phooooooone!

> (*She breaks down again.* **MAGGIE** *keeps rubbing her back; she can't help but laugh a little at* **OLIVIA**.)

> (**BILLY** *re-enters with toilet paper, hands some to* **OLIVIA**.)

*(To* **MAGGIE**.*)* Are you laughing at me?

**MAGGIE.** I'm sorry.

**OLIVIA.** I can't believe you're laughing at me!

**MAGGIE.** Well you know I find crying people funny, you know that about me.

> (**OLIVIA** *wipes her eyes with the toilet paper. Pause.*)

**OLIVIA.** Do you at least think I could come visit Carmike Falls, sometimes?

> (**BILLY** *looks at* **MAGGIE**. **MAGGIE** *looks back at him.*)

**MAGGIE.** Yeah, hon, of course.

(**BILLY** *and* **MAGGIE** *continue to look at each other.*)

(*Just then,* **WAYNE** *appears at the front door. He knocks, then opens it up.*)

**WAYNE.** Hi, uh –

(*He sees* **OLIVIA**.)

Sorry to interrupt –

(**OLIVIA** *pulls herself together.*)

**MAGGIE.** She's fine, don't worry about her.

**WAYNE.** You know where Joe is?

**MAGGIE.** He's upstairs in his room, I think, why?

**WAYNE.** I got a call from Jerry, who lives up near the entrance to Dodson? He said he thought he saw a couple people milling around a while ago. I went by, the elevator's not at the top. It's down there somewhere.

(*Short pause.*)

If I'm right, you guys are the only ones left with keys to that thing?

(*Pause.*)

**MAGGIE.** Well I'm sure he's –... Wayne, I know he wouldn't do that, he'd never –

**WAYNE.** Sure, but maybe you could check? Just to make certain?

(*Pause.* **MAGGIE** *heads upstairs.*)

**BILLY.** Sorry, you said... You said two people?

**WAYNE.** Yessir.

(*Pause.* **BILLY** *goes to the reception desk, picks up the portable phone, dials a number.*)

**MAGGIE.** (*Offstage, upstairs.*) JOE?!

(**BILLY** *holds the phone to his ear. He doesn't hear anything, he looks at it.*)

**BILLY.** I don't – it's not working –

(**OLIVIA** *goes to him.*)

**OLIVIA.** Oh you have to – that thing is messed up, you have to bang on the back to make it work –

(*She shows him.* **BILLY** *hits the back of the phone, he can hear now. He waits as it rings.*)

(**MAGGIE** *comes back downstairs, heading into the office.*)

**WAYNE.** At this point, it's condemned county property, so it would technically be trespassing. But the thing I'm more worried about is that old cribbing, it was falling apart even before it got shut down, it wouldn't take much for the roof in some of those tunnels to come down –

**BILLY.** (*Putting the phone down.*) It's just going to voicemail.

(**MAGGIE** *comes back out of the office.*)

**MAGGIE.** I don't know where he is, but I'm sure he didn't –

**WAYNE.** So the elevator keys are here?

(*Pause.* **MAGGIE** *goes to the cash box, opens it up. She looks.*)

They here?

(**MAGGIE** *doesn't respond.* **WAYNE** *grabs his radio.*)

(*Into his radio.*) Yeah, he's down there.

**BILLY.** (*To* **WAYNE.**) Wait, is Kel – is she down there with him? My granddaughter?

**WAYNE.** Not sure, sir. How old is your granddaughter?

**BILLY.** She's fourteen.

**MAGGIE.** (*Searching near the register.*) Where are my damn car keys?

**WAYNE.** / Woah, now, slow down –

**OLIVIA.** You're not thinking of going down there, are you?

**WAYNE.** We'll be sending a couple county guys over there to –

**MAGGIE.** I know those old tunnels better than anybody, I can –

> *(Just then, **JOE** comes in through the front door, carrying an empty water bottle. He stops when he sees everyone.)*
>
> *(Pause.)*

**JOE.** Hey.

> *(Pause.)*

What's going on?

**WAYNE.** *(Into his radio.)* Never mind, he's here.

> **(MAGGIE** *goes to* **JOE.)**

**MAGGIE.** Joe, thank God, are you okay?

**JOE.** Yeah, I'm fine –

**MAGGIE.** Where were you? Is Kel with you?

> *(Pause. **JOE** is petrified.)*

**JOE.** I don't know where she –... I was just wandering around town, I got a milkshake at the Lodge Café and –

**MAGGIE.** You're lying to me.

> *(Pause.)*

**JOE.** I'm not lying.

> **(BILLY** *goes to* **JOE.)**

**BILLY.** Wait, Joe, where's –? Were you with Kel?

> *(Pause.)*

**JOE.** I – I don't know –

**WAYNE.** You know that mine is condemned county property now, right? You realize you're not allowed / to –?

**JOE.** Yes.

**WAYNE.** And you realize that it would be *trespassing*, right? You understand what that means?

**JOE.** *Yes*, I know / what that –

**BILLY.** Did you take Kel down there?

**JOE.** She's fine –

**BILLY.** Then where is she?!

**JOE.** I don't –... She's *really fine* –

**MAGGIE.** Where are the elevator keys?

>            *(Pause.)*

**JOE.** I don't know.

**MAGGIE.** They're not in the cash box.

**JOE.** I said I *don't know.*

**MAGGIE.** What do you mean you don't know?!

**JOE.** Mom, I'm –. Look I'm not feeling very good, I just want to go lay down for a while –

>            *(He starts to head for the stairs,* **MAGGIE** *blocks him.)*

**MAGGIE.** Joe I'm not kidding around, if you took that girl down into that mine, you have to tell us where she is *right now* –

**JOE.** I don't know!

**MAGGIE.** Give me the keys.

**JOE.** Mom –

**MAGGIE.** Last chance. Give me the keys, *right now.*

**JOE.** *Mom, please!*

>            *(***MAGGIE** *thinks for a moment, then advances on* **JOE.** **JOE** *tries to move away from her, she forces her hands into his pockets.* **JOE** *tries to push her away.)*

/ *Mom stop!*

**OLIVIA.** / Maggie don't –

**WAYNE.** Okay now –

>            *(Finally,* **MAGGIE** *pulls a set of keys out of* **JOE**'s *pocket.)*

>            *(***MAGGIE** *stares at* **JOE** *in silence.* **JOE** *stares back at her.)*

>            *(Finally:)*

**BILLY.** Did you take her down there with you?

JOE. *She's fine!*

BILLY. Then *where is she*?!

JOE. I don't know, I –! Look, she's fine, but I can't tell you where she is –

BILLY. Why?! What does that mean?!

JOE. Look, she just wanted to see the bottom of the mine, / where the fire started –

MAGGIE. The *bottom*? You took her to the sixty-four-hundred level? No one's been down there in years, do you have any idea how dangerous it is down there?!

JOE. Yes, Mom! I know those tunnels, I know / what –!

MAGGIE. *And you took her down there with you?*

JOE. She asked me to –

MAGGIE. She's a fourteen-year-old girl! You're an adult, Joe!

JOE. Mom, please, just *shut up*!

> (MAGGIE *slaps* JOE *across the face, hard.*)

Mom, *please* –

MAGGIE. You know how easily you could have died down there?! *What is wrong with you?!*

> (JOE *is crumbling into himself. He stares at the floor.*)

JOE. I don't –... Mom...

OLIVIA. Okay, Maggie, he hears you –

MAGGIE. Back off, Livvy.

BILLY. Did you do anything to her down there?

JOE. No!

BILLY. Then just tell me where she is!

JOE. I can't, please –

> (*Suddenly,* BILLY *advances on* JOE.)

BILLY. *Tell me where she is,* / *right now* –

WAYNE. Okay –

> (*Just then,* **JOE** *looks up at* **BILLY**'s *face. As soon as he sees* **BILLY**'s *eyes, he jumps back like a frightened animal.* **BILLY** *stops dead, confused.*)

/ Woah –

**MAGGIE.** Joe –

> (**JOE** *moves to a corner of the room, pressing his back up against the wall. He stares straight at* **BILLY**'s *face, horrified.* **BILLY** *looks back at him, confused.*)

**BILLY.** What're you –?

> (**JOE** *covers his face with his hands. Pause.* **MAGGIE** *slowly goes to him.*)

**MAGGIE.** Joe, are you –? What's wrong?

**JOE.** Nothing, just please, get back, please don't –!

> (*He looks up at* **BILLY** *again for a moment. He closes his eyes, shakes his head a bit, then starts pounding his head with his fists.*)

I JUST DON'T FEEL GOOD, I DON'T –!

> (*Pause.*)

I need to go for a walk.

**MAGGIE.** No, *stay here –*

> (**BILLY**, *unsure of what to do, takes another step toward* **JOE**. **JOE** *looks up and sees him, panicking. He dashes for the front door, running outside.*)

Joe –!

> (**JOE** *is gone.* **WAYNE** *goes to the front door, watching him go.*)
>
> (*Silence. Everyone breathes.*)

**WAYNE.** I'm gonna go look for her.

**BILLY.** I'll go with you.

> (**WAYNE** *turns to* **BILLY**.)

**WAYNE.** Sir, I think it'd be best if you just stay here –

**BILLY.** I'm not going to just stay here and sit on my hands –

**MAGGIE.** *(To* **BILLY.***)* Joe really wouldn't have done anything, I swear to you –

**BILLY.** *(Sharp.) You don't know that, Maggie, you –...!*

> *(Pause.)*

I'm going with you.

> *(Short pause.)*

**WAYNE.** Okay then.

> (**BILLY** *and* **WAYNE** *make their way outside.* **MAGGIE** *and* **OLIVIA** *watch them go.)*
>
> *(Pause.)*

**MAGGIE.** Livvy, could you –...? I'm sure she's fine, but maybe you could just look around for her too.

**OLIVIA.** Sure, Maggie.

**MAGGIE.** Joe said she was fine, he wouldn't have done anything, he –...

> *(Pause.* **OLIVIA** *looks at* **MAGGIE**, *unsure of what to say.)*

**OLIVIA.** I'll drive around a bit. I'll call if I find her, okay?

**MAGGIE.** Thank you.

> (**OLIVIA** *heads toward the door, then stops, turns to* **MAGGIE**.*)*

**OLIVIA.** Joe was seeing it again. When Billy was looking at him, he was seeing the face.

> *(Pause.)*

**MAGGIE.** There were a lot of people coming at him, it might just be –. There was a lot going on.

**OLIVIA.** He was, Maggie, you know he was.

> *(Pause.)*

When he attacked Cam, I told you to have him committed, for his good *and* yours. And I wasn't the only one around here saying that. So if he's seeing those things / again –

**MAGGIE.** Livvy, it's / not like that –

**OLIVIA.** I'm looking out for you, Maggie. That's all.

> *(Pause.)*

I'll drive around a bit. I'll call if I find her, okay?

> *(She turns and exits.* **MAGGIE** *is left alone.)*

# ACT THREE

## Scene One

*(Night.* **JOE** *is sitting on the ground, outside, lost in thought.)*

*(Upstairs,* **MAGGIE** *is sitting on the couch in the living room, alone, watching TV.)*

*(After a moment, a bright flashlight beam is focused on* **JOE**'s *face. He squints, shielding his eyes from the light with his hand.)*

*(***WAYNE*** enters, shining a flashlight into* **JOE**'s *face. He approaches* **JOE**, *standing over him.)*

**JOE.** I'm not doing anything wrong.

**WAYNE.** Didn't say you were.

*(He approaches* **JOE**, *turning off his flashlight. He looks out.)*

God, I've never seen the town this dark. With all the streetlamps turned off, kinda creepy.

*(Looking up.)*

Without the lights, you can sure see a ton of stars though. God almighty.

*(Pause.)*

**JOE.** Are you gonna arrest me?

*(Pause.* **WAYNE** *keeps looking up into the sky.)*

**WAYNE.** Nah, Joe, I'm not gonna...

*(Pause.)*

When I was a kid, my little brother Jamie and I, we used to spend hours out here, looking up at the sky during the night. He would always ask me questions about stars, space, whathaveyou, I had no idea of course but I wanted to sound smart so I made up all kinds of shit. Told him once that shooting stars were from astronauts who were up there working on satellites, flicking their cigarette butts out the window.

> *(He chuckles. He looks up. Pause.)*

**JOE.** Did you find her?

**WAYNE.** Oh yeah, hours ago. Sitting down by the river, just listening to music or something. 'Course, you knew that already.

> *(Pause.)*

Why didn't you tell us where she was, Joe?

**JOE.** She asked me not to.

> *(Pause. **WAYNE** sits down on the ground next to **JOE**.)*

**WAYNE.** You probably think that I don't like you.

> *(**JOE** looks at **WAYNE**.)*

**JOE.** No, I know for *certain* that you don't like me. You've never liked me. You were always stopping me when I was a kid for no reason.

**WAYNE.** Oh – no reason, is that right? So you never smoked weed in that alley behind the car dealership, huh?

**JOE.** That was *one time* –

**WAYNE.** I never had to go to the high school because you locked yourself in the janitor's closet, or –?

**JOE.** *Okay.* I get it.

> *(Pause.)*

**WAYNE.** I don't dislike you, Joe. I honestly don't.

> *(Pause.)*

My dad was a cop here in town before me, do you remember that?

**JOE.** No.

**WAYNE**. I guess he would have been retiring when you were still pretty young. Was the only cop in Clements his whole life, he loved it. Everyone in town knew him, trusted him with their lives. 'Course, town like this – he wasn't dealing with anything too major. Mostly traffic violations. Some vandalism here and there. Once every couple years he'd get a grand larceny call, that was like Christmas. Only time he really hit a wall, though, was with this guy who lived here in town, guy named Dave Ellis, lived up past that ridge there.

*(He points.)*

You ever heard of this guy?

**JOE**. No.

**WAYNE**. Weird, weird guy. He was a Vietnam vet, I think he had seen some stuff, came back a little messed up, you know. But, he wasn't doing anything illegal per se, he'd barely interact with anyone in town at all, so it was fine. Live and let live, that's what it was like back then.

**JOE**. Why are you telling me / this?

**WAYNE**. No but wait for it. After a while, he started getting a little –... It started innocently enough. He'd come down into town, he'd go into the grocery store or the 13 Club and say something weird, most people just laughed it off. Gradually he started coming into town more often, sayin' weirder and weirder stuff. But – people were respectful, they gave him his distance.

*(Pause.)*

My brother Jamie and I were walking home one night, beautiful summer night. I was probably nine, so that makes Jamie about six. We were almost home, and then all of a sudden we round a corner, and there's Dave Ellis, just standing there, in the middle of the street. Staring at the two of us. We had no idea what to do, so we just kept walkin'. And we were almost past him, when suddenly he grabs Jamie like –

*(He demonstrates with his hands.)*

**WAYNE.** And he looks at him and says, "You don't even fucking know. You'll never fucking know."

*(Short pause.)*

I remember that, those exact words: "You don't even fucking know. You'll never fucking know."

*(Pause.)*

**JOE.** What did that mean?

**WAYNE.** Didn't mean anything, he was nuts.

*(Pause.)*

But anyway that's all he said. Then he lets my brother go, and Jamie's peed himself by this point because he's six years old and he's scared out of his brain. And so we both run home and tell our dad what happened. And he left the house, right then.

*(Short pause.)*

**JOE.** Did he arrest him?

**WAYNE.** No, Joe, he didn't arrest him.

*(Pause.)*

See this is the thing, nowadays you'd have to call up the state and they'd send a social worker, put him in some crappy program that we're paying for with our tax dollars, then a few months later he'd be back on the streets, grabbing some other six-year-old and saying the same crazy shit. That's the world we live in today.

*(Pause.)*

**JOE.** Wait, so what did your dad...?

**WAYNE.** He found him on the streets, took him back to his property on that ridge over there, and beat the living shit out of him. Broke his jaw in two places. And from then on? Dave Ellis kept to himself except for an occasional trip to the grocery store to use his pension check. And he was *perfectly* polite when he did so.

*(Silence.* **JOE** *looks at* **WAYNE***.)*

**JOE**. Are you gonna...?

> (**WAYNE** *looks at* **JOE**.)

**WAYNE**. What, me? No, God, Joe, that's not what I'm saying, geez. I'd never do that. I'd be fired, anyway.

> (*Pause.*)

**JOE**. So why are you...?

**WAYNE**. You feel like you're gonna stay here in town for good?

> (*Pause.*)

**JOE**. Mom mentioned something about us maybe moving.

> (*Pause.* **WAYNE** *looks at him.*)

**WAYNE**. She did?

> (*Pause.*)

Where to?

> (**JOE** *shrugs. Short pause.*)

Here's the thing – if you move somewhere else? You're just gonna be someone else's problem. Some other cop. And they might not know you like I do. They may be more prone to deal with you like my father dealt with Dave Ellis if you're doing stupid shit like coaxing little girls down into mine shafts.

**JOE**. I didn't –! I didn't do that!

**WAYNE**. You do anything to her down there, Joe?

**JOE**. No, I didn't!

**WAYNE**. You can tell me, I'm on your side –

**JOE**. *I didn't do anything.*

**WAYNE**. So why'd you take her down there then?

**JOE**. She asked me to.

> (*Pause.*)

**WAYNE**. Hm.

> (*Pause.*)

I'm not a bad guy, Joe. And I'm not out to get you, I'm here to protect you. But I just want you to know – if you decide to stay here in town? I'm gonna watch you like a hawk. And it's for your own good. And your mom's. You understand?

> *(Pause.* **JOE** *looks at him.)*

Tell me that you understand, Joe.

**JOE.** I understand.

**WAYNE.** There we go.

> *(He looks back up to the sky. Silence.)*

**JOE.** *(Small.)* I'm sorry.

**WAYNE.** Hm?

**JOE.** I'm sorry.

**WAYNE.** No one got hurt –

**JOE.** No I mean –...

> *(Pause.)*

I'm sorry I'm back.

> *(Pause.)*

I'm sorry you have to deal with me.

> *(****WAYNE*** *pats* **JOE***'s shoulder.)*

**WAYNE.** Aw, now.

> *(Pause. He gets up.)*

You should go inside. Your mom's probably worried.

**JOE.** I think I might just sit here for a while longer –

**WAYNE.** Joe.

**JOE.** It's okay, we talked about this, when I feel overwhelmed, I can take walks and I –

**WAYNE.** *Joe.*

> *(Short pause.)*

You should go inside now.

> *(****JOE*** *looks up at* **WAYNE.** **WAYNE** *stares at him.)*

## Scene Two

(**MAGGIE** *is still alone in the living room, watching TV.*)

(*After a moment,* **JOE** *appears at the front door. He slips in his keys and opens up the door.*)

(**MAGGIE** *hears him. She turns off the TV, waiting for a moment.*)

(**JOE** *closes the door and takes a few steps inside.* **MAGGIE** *comes out of the living room, descends the stairs.*)

(**MAGGIE** *and* **JOE** *see one another. A silence.*)

JOE. They found her, you know. She's fine, she was just –

MAGGIE. Wayne called me, I know. You could have just *told* us where she was, Joe, you –...

(*Pause.*)

I'm sorry I flew off the handle like that.

JOE. I deserved it.

MAGGIE. You deserved me getting mad, but not like that –

JOE. I deserved more than that, really.

(*Pause.*)

MAGGIE. When Billy was coming at you, earlier? Did you see...? On Billy, did you see the face?

(*Short pause.*)

Do you think you're gonna see him that way for good now? Or was that just...?

(*Pause.* **JOE** *looks away.*)

JOE. I don't know, Mom, I –.

(*Pause.*)

I'm sure it's fine. I was just upset, everyone was shouting at me.

MAGGIE. Yeah, maybe it's –.

*(Pause.)*

**MAGGIE.** Christ, Joe, why did you take that girl down into the mine? I know you, Joe, I know you better than you think, and I know you're smarter than this, you *know* you shouldn't have –

**JOE.** What if I'm not? What if I'm not smarter than this, what if I'm just really fucked up?

**MAGGIE.** Okay, / don't –

**JOE.** I'm serious. What if this is just me, this is who I am? What if you just have a son who's sort of fucked up?

**MAGGIE.** Joe, please stop / saying –

**JOE.** Would you be okay with that?

> *(Silence.* **MAGGIE** *doesn't know how to respond. She looks away.)*

You know how in high school, I used to make you those ashtrays in my art class?

**MAGGIE.** I – remember you making stuff –

**JOE.** No, not stuff, just ashtrays, like a ton of them. I was in like, eighth grade, I think? The school had just gotten one of those... The big ovens that get really hot and cook the clay?

**MAGGIE.** A kiln.

**JOE.** Yeah, the school had just gotten a kiln and the art teacher was so excited, she said that all semester we could make whatever we wanted. So the first day I wanted to try something really simple, so I just made this little ashtray. And I brought it home and I gave it to you, and you were like, "Oh this is so neat! Thank you so much!" It was right around the time that Dad had left, right after. And I was like – I just made her happy.

**MAGGIE.** Yeah, I – I remember that.

**JOE.** And so the next day I got to make something else, and I thought – well, she loved the ashtray, I'll make her another one. That made her so happy, I'll just keep making her happy. And so every few days I'd make you a new ashtray and give it to you, and you'd smile and say thank you, and everyone at school was making fun of me for doing nothing but ashtrays, my art teacher was treating me like there was something wrong with me. But I thought – it doesn't matter, I don't care what everyone else thinks, I'm making her happy.

**MAGGIE**. Joe.

**JOE**. And then like months later, I brought you another ashtray, and it was probably the twentieth one I'd made you, and finally you looked at me and you were like – "You need to stop. You're being weird."

> *(Pause.)*

And all of a sudden I was like – oh. Wait – those kids at school, my art teacher – they're right. This is weird, I'm being weird. How did I not understand that this was weird?

**MAGGIE**. You were just trying to be sweet –

**JOE**. But this is the thing, this is what keeps happening to me, I try to do like, one thing right, and I'm sure that I'm doing the right thing, I'm sure that I'm on track. And then there's always this moment where I look up and someone looks at me and they're like – "You're being weird."

> *(Pause.)*

I'm – *so* tired of being weird, Mom.

> *(Pause. **JOE** starts to become upset. **MAGGIE** goes to him, wrapping her arms around him.)*

I'm sorry.

**MAGGIE**. Okay, now. Enough of that, okay? You've just been dealt a – difficult hand in life, that's all it is.

**JOE**. But why can't I just figure out how to live life like a normal person?

**MAGGIE**. Hell, if I knew the answer to that question, don't you think I'd tell you? Things'll get better from here on out, you've got your psychiatrist now, you'll get over this –

**JOE**. But what if I don't get over this? What if we leave town and I just get worse?

> (**MAGGIE** *doesn't know how to respond.*)
>
> (*Pause.* **JOE** *goes to the pocket watch, picking it up, looking at it.*)

Your dad would be so ashamed of me if he were alive today. He'd be so ashamed that he was related to me.

> (**MAGGIE** *goes to* **JOE**, *taking the watch out of his hand and putting it back on the shelf. She goes to* **JOE**, *grabbing him.*)

**MAGGIE**. All I can tell you, Joe, is that you're going to be *fine*. We're both going to be *fine*.

> (*Short pause.*)

Right?

> (**JOE** *looks at her.*)
>
> (*Just then,* **BILLY** *appears at the front door.* **MAGGIE** *sees him through the window,* **JOE** *doesn't notice.* **MAGGIE** *signals for* **BILLY** *to hold on.*)

If you get to bed now you'll get a few decent hours before light.

(*Rubbing* **JOE***'s back a bit.*) You feel a little better?

**JOE**. I –...

> (*He looks at* **MAGGIE**. *A silence as he stares at her.*)
>
> (*Finally:*)

Yeah, Mom.

**MAGGIE**. Good.

> (*Short pause.*)

You're gonna be fine. I'll make sure of it. That's my job.

> (**JOE** *looks at her for a moment, then gets up, heading upstairs.*)

*(MAGGIE signals for BILLY to wait for a second. She watches JOE go all the way upstairs, disappear into his bedroom.)*

*(She goes to the front door. She puts a finger up to her lips, signaling BILLY to be quiet. She opens up the door.)*

Keep quiet, okay?

**BILLY**. Sure.

*(He comes inside. MAGGIE gently closes the door behind him. They speak in hushed tones throughout the scene.)*

I couldn't sleep. I thought I'd come back here, wait until dawn. Thought I'd try and catch you before Joe woke up.

**MAGGIE**. Where're you staying?

**BILLY**. The Super 8 in Kellogg.

**MAGGIE**. And Kel, she's –?

**BILLY**. Oh, she's fine. Didn't even take twenty minutes to find her. All that fuss over nothing.

*(Pause. They both sit down on chairs in the front area, near the cash register.)*

**MAGGIE**. I'm so sorry, Billy –

**BILLY**. It's okay.

**MAGGIE**. Honestly, if I thought Joe was capable of something like that, I wouldn't have let him hang around Kel –

**BILLY**. Kel is – a mature kid. She played her part in it too.

*(Pause.)*

She said she really liked it, said that Joe was really nice to her. Said she was happy to see the bottom of the mine, where that fire started. She's a little morbid, you know.

**MAGGIE**. Well, that's the age.

**BILLY**. Hm.

*(Pause.)*

**BILLY**. It's hard, you know. I didn't expect to become a parent again. I always figured by this point Sue and I would be doing the grandparent thing. Babysitting a bit, giving too many presents, missing most of the bad parts.

**MAGGIE**. At least you have a grandkid. I somehow doubt that's ever gonna happen for me.

(*Pause.*)

It's strange, thinking that families can just – stop. My sister doesn't have any kids, no cousins. After all that's come before me, generations of Bunkers, it might just stop with this one below me.

**BILLY**. You and Caleb ever think of having more than one kid?

**MAGGIE**. It was hard enough to have the one. And I was no spring chicken when I got pregnant with him, you know. Thirty-seven.

**BILLY**. Not that old.

**MAGGIE**. Well. I guess it wasn't in the cards for us to have a lot of kids. To be honest, part of it was the – making part. I've never been all that interested in sex, and turns out Caleb wasn't interested in someone with my particular equipment. I mean not that I'm opposed to it or anything, I was just never that excited by it.

**BILLY**. Sue wasn't either.

**MAGGIE**. Oh yeah?

**BILLY**. Anyway that prostate cancer I had in my forties left me impotent, so it wasn't really on the menu anyway.

(**MAGGIE** *smiles.*)

(*Pause.*)

**MAGGIE**. Caleb always made noises.

**BILLY**. What's that?

(**MAGGIE** *gives him a look.*)

Oh.

**MAGGIE**. Yeah. I think he was overcompensating.

**BILLY**. Oh, no.

**MAGGIE**. Yep. Like a bad actor in some low-budget porno movie. All these grunts.

> (**BILLY** *laughs nearly out loud.* **MAGGIE** *shushes him.*)
>
> (*Pause.*)

**BILLY**. Sue used to make me keep my shirt on.

**MAGGIE**. Why?

**BILLY**. She thought my nipples looked strange.

> (*Pause.*)

**MAGGIE**. Well do they?

**BILLY**. Oh I think they're just fine.

> (**MAGGIE** *looks at* **BILLY**. **BILLY** *pulls his collar out, letting* **MAGGIE** *look down his shirt.*)

**MAGGIE**. I can't see anything.

> (*She goes behind the reception desk, taking a mining helmet off of the wall. She turns on the helmet lamp.* **BILLY** *stifles a laugh.*)
>
> (**MAGGIE** *goes to* **BILLY**, *looking down his shirt.*)

Oh I think they're fine.

**BILLY**. Thank you!

**MAGGIE**. They're a little small but they're just fine.

> (*She turns off the headlamp. She looks at* **BILLY**, *smiles at him. She takes the helmet off, puts it on the counter.*)
>
> (*Then, she grabs* **BILLY** *by the hand and starts to lead him upstairs. She puts a finger to her lips, indicating for him to be quiet.*)
>
> (*She silently leads* **BILLY** *upstairs to her bedroom, careful not to make any noise.* **BILLY** *enters the bedroom first,* **MAGGIE** *shuts the door behind him.*)
>
> (**MAGGIE** *motions to the bed. They keep their voices low.*)

**MAGGIE.** Go ahead.

**BILLY.** Did you have a side?

**MAGGIE.** I don't even remember now.

**BILLY.** I was on the left.

**MAGGIE.** Fine.

> (**BILLY** *gets into bed, lying down.* **MAGGIE** *lies down beside him. They stare up at the ceiling, not touching.*)
>
> (*Pause.*)

This is nice.

**BILLY.** Sure.

> (*Pause.*)

Haven't been in the same bed with anyone in years.

**MAGGIE.** Over a decade for me.

> (*Short pause.*)

How big is that house of yours?

**BILLY.** Not too big. Three-bedroom. Third bedroom is full of old junk but I can clear it out.

**MAGGIE.** Big enough for four people?

**BILLY.** Should be.

> (*Pause.*)

**MAGGIE.** Billy, are you sure you're all right with Joe...? He really scared me today.

**BILLY.** He's not dangerous, right? He just got a little overwhelmed.

> (*Pause.*)

**MAGGIE.** Livvy's youngest son Cam – when he was younger he used to spend most days during the summer riding his bike around town. One day, Cam said something to Joe. I don't know what, taunting him. I never liked the kid truth be told. And Joe couldn't see him, you know, he could only see the face.

> (*Pause.*)

Joe didn't mean to hurt him. He just got scared, pushed
him off his bike. But Cam fell in this certain way, and –...
He had to wear a cast for a bit. Livvy was out of her
mind about it.

>*(Pause.)*

**BILLY**. It was just once.

**MAGGIE**. I don't know, Billy, he –... Kel and Joe were together
for one day and they wound up at the bottom of that
mine, what is he gonna do when they're living together?

>*(Pause.)*

Maybe we're just being selfish.

>*(Pause.)*

**BILLY**. Joe'll be fine, Maggie. He's got a great mother to
support him.

**MAGGIE**. Not so great.

>*(Pause. **MAGGIE** starts to become upset.)*

**BILLY**. You've done everything for that kid. Without you
he'd still be out on the streets up in Alaska.

**MAGGIE**. I could've done more.

>*(She sits up in bed, trying to calm down. **BILLY**
>sits up as well.)*

**BILLY**. Most parents would've given up by now –

**MAGGIE**. *I could've done more.*

>*(Pause. **BILLY** looks at her.)*

When I finally decided to fly up there and look for
him... For years, we had a deal. He'd call me collect
every Sunday, same time. And he kept to it. For a long
time I convinced myself he was okay even though the
calls were getting weirder, but then, last winter – the
calls stopped. I called Caleb for help, he told me Joe
was an adult now, whatever mistakes he made were
his own. Finally I couldn't stand it, flew up there to
look for him myself. I got up there and Anchorage was

bigger than I thought. Middle of the winter – night all the time, only about four hours of light a day.

*(Pause.)*

A couple days after I got there, I was walking around these streets downtown – middle of the afternoon and pitch-black out – and I saw this man, this guy wrapped up in what looked like tarps draped over a bunch of old winter coats, sitting on the ground outside of this liquor store. I hoped to God it wasn't him, but when I went up to him, I could see my dad's old pocket watch hanging off his belt. I lifted up the tarp so I could see his face, and when he looked at me – he was terrified. I could tell he couldn't see me, he could only see the face. He didn't even know who I was.

*(Pause.)*

And right at that second, I thought to myself – what the hell am I gonna do with him? Force him to come with me, try to clean him up in my little hotel room? Put another plane ticket on my credit card, force him to come back here? Hope he doesn't push any more kids off their bikes?

*(Pause.)*

Or – I could just turn around. Go back to my hotel. Get on the plane, come back to Clements. Live my own life, without that burden.

**BILLY**. But – you didn't do it. You took care of him –

**MAGGIE**. Three days later.

*(Pause.)*

I went back to my hotel room and did nothing for three days. Barely did anything, just watched TV, ate at the Perkins on the corner, tried to forget I'd even seen him. Each night the temperature was falling lower and lower... Finally I called the police, told them a homeless man needed medical attention.

*(Pause.)*

On my way to the hospital to get him, I kept thinking – maybe I shouldn't have made that call. Maybe that would have just been easier for everyone.

*(Pause.)*

What kind of mother could do all that?

*(Pause.)*

**BILLY**. I've been watching Patrick fall apart for a few years now, Maggie. Sometimes it's hard to figure out the best way to help him –

**MAGGIE**. Billy, I almost left him there –

**BILLY**. But you didn't. That's what's important, you didn't leave him there.

*(Pause.)*

**MAGGIE**. You know he's what's most important to me, Billy. Seeing him in that hospital bed, nearly dead... I couldn't believe I waited that long. I realized – I don't know what I'd do without him.

*(Short pause.)*

We can only go down there as long as it's good for him. That's it.

*(Pause.)*

**BILLY**. With all we've dealt with? We can handle it. We can handle it together.

*(Pause. **MAGGIE** looks at him.)*

**MAGGIE**. Yeah.

*(Then, **BILLY** goes to her, wrapping his arms around her. They hold one another for a few moments in silence.)*

**BILLY**. It's a nice little house I've got out there. Looks over the river.

*(Short pause.)*

**MAGGIE**. What side of town?

**BILLY**. Franklin Street.

**MAGGIE.** The good side.

**BILLY.** Yep. Got a nice yard, little patio in the back. They closed the grocery store across the street last year so there's not a lot of light pollution. On clear nights you can see the galaxy.

  *(Pause.)*

**MAGGIE.** This could be nice. This could work.

**BILLY.** Yes it could.

**MAGGIE.** Only took us fifty goddam years.

  (**BILLY** *smiles. They hold one another for a few more moments.)*

**BILLY.** I should get back to the hotel before Kel wakes up.

**MAGGIE.** Sure.

  (**BILLY** *stands up, getting out of bed.)*

**BILLY.** Does the front door lock behind me?

**MAGGIE.** Don't worry about it.

**BILLY.** Okay.

  *(Pause.)*

I'll stop by tomorrow morning, before we head up to Moscow. And we can make plans?

**MAGGIE.** Yep. We'll make plans.

  (**BILLY** *smiles at her.)*

## Scene Three

*(That same night, nearing dawn. **MAGGIE** is asleep in her bedroom. The stage is nearly black.)*

*(After a moment, **JOE** appears in the hallway, unslept. He descends the stairs, making his way into the museum, looking around.)*

*(Upstairs, **MAGGIE** stirs in her bed a little. **JOE** hears her, looking up toward the stairs.)*

*(**MAGGIE** settles down. **JOE** waits for a few moments.)*

*(**JOE** goes to the pocket watch on the shelf. He stares at it, motionless, for what feels like an irrationally long time.)*

*(Then, **JOE** makes his way toward the office. He opens up the door carefully, then goes inside, shutting the door behind him, not turning on the light.)*

*(About twelve seconds of complete silence.)*

*(Then, a gunshot in the office. A flash of light underneath the door. The sound of an object hitting the floor.)*

*(**MAGGIE** wakes up, unsure if the sound was real or in a dream.)*

*(We begin to hear the sound of **JOE**, in the office, choking on his own blood.)*

*(The choking sounds continue as **MAGGIE** becomes more aware, realizes that the sound wasn't in her dream.)*

**MAGGIE.** Joe?

*(She gets out of bed, making her way into the hallway.)*

Joe, what was that?!

*(She heads down the stairs, coming to the ground floor.)*

*(Finally, she becomes aware of the choking sounds. She rushes toward the office, opening the door, going inside. She turns on a light in the office.)*

*(She lets out a scream.)*

**MAGGIE**. *(Offstage.)* JOE?! WHAT ARE YOU DOING, WHAT DID YOU –?!

*(Short pause.)*

*(Offstage.)* Oh my God, oh God, okay – give that to me! GIVE THAT TO ME, NOW!

*(We hear the sound of **MAGGIE** struggling with **JOE** as he continues to choke.)*

*(**MAGGIE** re-enters, holding a small pistol in her hand that is covered in blood. She panics for a moment, not knowing what to do. She rushes toward the front desk, putting the gun on a shelf below the register. She grabs the portable phone.)*

*(She turns on the phone, dialing 9-1-1.)*

*(She puts the phone to her ear. She doesn't hear anything. She realizes the phone isn't working again.)*

*Dammit, I'm –*

*(She looks at the phone, pressing on the back, trying to make it work. She puts it back to her ear. Nothing. **JOE** continues to choke in the background.)*

*(Exploding.)* GODDAMMIT!

*(She hits the back of the phone with her palm. The back shatters, the battery falls to the floor.)*

NO! NO NO NO!

*(She picks up the battery, realizes the phone is broken. She thinks for a quick moment, then rushes to the front door, opening it up, screaming outside.)*

ANYONE! PLEASE, HELP, ANYONE!

*(Short pause, looking around.)*

CAN ANYONE HEAR ME?!

*(She looks. There isn't anyone.)*

*(She rushes back into the main room, unsure of what to do. She runs back to the office door, seeing* **JOE**. *She looks away, horrified.)*

JOE, I CAN'T –! I DON'T KNOW WHAT TO DO, I DON'T KNOW WHAT TO DO!

*(She stands in the middle of the space, in a panicked daze, as* **JOE** *continues to choke.)*

*(Pause.)*

Caleb?!

*(Short pause.)*

CALEB!

*(She looks up the stairs, toward the office, back toward the front door.)*

*(Senseless, wilting.)* Dad?

*(Silence apart from* **JOE**'s *choking.)*

*(A few moments pass.* **JOE**'s *choking is starting to get quieter and quieter.)*

*(A few more moments.)*

*(Finally, silence.)*

*(***MAGGIE** *goes to the office door. She looks at* **JOE** *for a moment, then shuts the door, sitting on the ground, her back up against the door.)*

*(She sits in silence, breathing. She buries her face in her knees.)*

## Scene Four

*(Then, as in the beginning of the play, a single light comes on. We see that it's emanating from a miner's helmet on top of* **JOE***'s head.* **JOE** *looks over the audience for a moment.)*

*(***MAGGIE***, still at the door, remains visible throughout the scene.)*

**JOE**. Sixty-four-hundred level. All the way down. Just under 6,500 feet below the surface of the earth, well over a mile down.

*(Pause.)*

Temperatures down here are around a-hundred and fifteen normally. This is where the fire started, in 1972. Started right over there, they think, though no one on this level survived so they aren't certain.

*(Pause.)*

Around one in the morning, up on thirty-seven-hundred level, they started smelling smoke. Didn't think much of it at first, a lot of these guys would smoke on their breaks. By the time they finally got inside here – the fire was so hot that everyone had turned to ash. Nothing here but wedding rings, some equipment, belt buckles. My grandpa's watch.

*(Pause.)*

That all happened. Right here. And at the time – no one even realized it was happening.

*(Pause.)*

It's really hot down here.

*(Pause.)*

We should probably go back up.

**KEL**. *(In the darkness.)* No.

*(***JOE** *turns, the light from his headlamp illuminating* **KEL***'s face.)*

**JOE**. This is it, Kel. There's nothing more to see. This is all the way down.

>       *(Pause.)*

>   It's hot. Let's go.

>       *(Pause.* **KEL** *stares forward.)*

**KEL**. No.

**JOE**. Kel, I'm serious. Get back in the elevator, we're / going –

**KEL**. You can go, but I'm staying here.

**JOE**. It doesn't work like that. Once I take the elevator up, you can't call it back down.

**KEL**. So leave me down here.

>       *(Short pause.* **JOE** *takes a step toward* **KEL**, **KEL** *moves away from him.)*

>   Don't.

**JOE**. Stop fooling around, Kel.

**KEL**. I'm not.

**JOE**. C'mon, it's hot, just get back in the / elevator –

**KEL**. *Just leave me here.* You said that no one comes down here anymore so no one will even find me. I'm sorry, I know it's unfair of me to do this to you right now, but I can't go back up there, I'm not –

**JOE**. Why?!

**KEL**. I can't do it anymore! I can't go to Moscow to do the stupid mock legislature, I can't go back home to deal with my dad, it would be a lot easier for everyone if you just left me down here.

**JOE**. You'd die down here!

**KEL**. *I know!*

>       *(Pause.)*

>   Do you have any idea what the next five years for me are gonna be like? My dad is gonna get worse, I *hate* the kids in my school, my grandpa's dying and he won't even tell me!

**JOE**. He's –?

**KEL.** He has cancer. And it's bad. I overheard him talking to his doctor on the phone.

**JOE.** Well – people get over cancer!

**KEL.** No, I heard the way he was talking about it. So he's gonna die, then I'm just gonna be back with my dad, and I can't do that. I'm not going to do that, I *can't* do that –

**JOE.** But you're only like thirteen years old!

**KEL.** I'm fourteen!

**JOE.** You've only got a few years left in the house anyway, then you can move out, like you said last night, go any place you wanted –

**KEL.** That's never going to happen –

**JOE.** Why not?

**KEL.** *Because I'm just going to turn out like you!*

　　　　*(Pause.)*

　　Please, just – leave me down here.

　　　　*(Silence.)*

**JOE.** What are you gonna do after this?

　　　　*(Short pause.)*

　　I mean just tell me, like, what you're going to do today. What are you going to do after we go back up?

**KEL.** *I don't want / to go back –*

**JOE.** I know, I know! I'm just saying, if you went back up, then what would happen?

　　　　*(Pause.)*

**KEL.** I'd just go back to my grandpa.

**JOE.** Then what?

**KEL.** I don't know! We'd go to Moscow tomorrow. I'd do my stupid bill about Carmike Falls Day.

**JOE.** Then what?

　　　　*(Pause.)*

**KEL**. I'd go back home. My grandpa would start getting sick. I'd have to watch.

**JOE**. Maybe. And maybe then he'd die.

**KEL**. What?

**JOE**. And then you'd have to go live with your dad.

**KEL**. Stop it.

**JOE**. And he'll keep drinking. Maybe he'll even get worse. And then things could get *really* bad –

**KEL**. Shut up!

**JOE**. But then what? What about after that?

> (*Pause.* **KEL** *thinks.*)

**KEL**. I'd probably just get stuck in Carmike Falls, get some shitty job –

**JOE**. Or you go to college?

> (*Pause.*)

Say you go to college, say you get your degree in law or something –

**KEL**. I don't wanna be a lawyer!

**JOE**. Well I don't know, I barely know you! What would you study, then?!

**KEL**. I don't know, I...

> (*Pause.*)

Maybe like – history?

**JOE**. Yes! Okay. So you study history. You get your degree or whatever, and you become a teacher!

**KEL**. But that doesn't even sound all that great, and that's like the *best-case scenario* –

> (**JOE** *goes to* **KEL***, the light shining directly in her face.*)

**JOE**. I'm not saying it's great, I'm not trying to make you feel better, I'm just saying you don't get to not try. And it's not about you, it's not about your happiness, it's about you being a smart person who gets good grades so it's your, like, *obligation* to try.

(*Pause.*)

I wasn't smart, I was born with nothing but problems. You're lucky.

(*Silence.*)

KEL. What if I don't want to try?

JOE. I don't care. You have to. You have to because maybe one day you'll be a teacher, and you'll take one of your students down into some mine shaft or something, and they'll start freaking out and ask you to leave them down there, and you have to talk them out of it.

(*Pause.*)

KEL. I really doubt that's ever going to happen?

JOE. Or something like it! You get what I'm saying.

(*Silence.* KEL *starts to calm down.*)

KEL. It's really hot down here.

JOE. Yeah.

(*Pause.*)

You want water?

(*He goes to* KEL, *hands her his water bottle. She takes a long drink.*)

(*Pause.*)

KEL. It could be like that, or it could just be really shitty, you know. My future could just be really shitty.

(*Pause.*)

JOE. Yeah, maybe.

(*Silence.* KEL *takes a breath.*)

KEL. If I go back up with you... Do you think you could just give me some space?

JOE. Yeah, sure.

KEL. Seriously, I really just need some time by myself –

**JOE.** I get it –

**KEL.** Just a couple hours, I can't be around my grandpa right now, or your mom, I just –

**JOE.** *Kel. I get it.* I promise I won't tell anyone where you are.

(*Pause.*)

So can we *please* go back up now?

(*Pause.*)

(*Finally,* **KEL** *exits.* **JOE** *follows her.*)

## Scene Five

*(Lights come back up on the museum.)*

*(Early morning, a few hours after the end of Scene Three.* **MAGGIE** *is in the same position, her back up against the closed office door. She is in a state of partial sleep, barely aware, in a daze.)*

*(***BILLY*** *appears at the front door, holding two gas station coffees. He struggles to open the door with his elbows.)*

**BILLY**. *(Calling out.)* Maggie?

*(***MAGGIE*** *hears him, waking up fully. She stands up, a bit disoriented. She looks back to the office door, then back to* **BILLY**.*)*

*(***BILLY*** *finally manages to open up the door. He sees* **MAGGIE**, *going to her.)*

Oh – morning. I'm glad I caught you. Kel's outside, suddenly she's all excited about giving her speech tomorrow, she wants to get there early so she can practice a few times.

*(He goes to* **MAGGIE**, *looking at her. She looks at him, dreamlike.)*

**MAGGIE**. Kel's here?

**BILLY**. Yeah, just in the truck there. Didn't sleep too well?

*(Pause.)*

**MAGGIE**. No.

**BILLY**. I didn't sleep much either, tried to sleep when I got back to the hotel, my mind was going a mile a minute. Figured you wouldn't get much either.

*(He offers* **MAGGIE** *a coffee. She takes it.)*

I don't wanna keep you too much, and I know Kel's anxious to get a move on, but...

*(He pulls a truck stop newspaper out of his jacket. It's open to the classifieds.)*

I was just thinking, we're gonna be down in Moscow for the next couple days, probably drive back to Carmike Falls on Thursday, maybe Friday. And you know – we could easily swing back by here. And it got me thinking...

*(He points to an ad in the classifieds.* **MAGGIE** *looks.)*

It looks like a decent trailer, and two hundred is a fair price. I thought – maybe we could start bringing some of your stuff down to Carmike Falls. Enough to get you settled, at least.

*(***MAGGIE** *turns away from* **BILLY***, looking toward the office door.* **BILLY** *finally senses something is off.)*

Or – if you wanted to stick around here a while longer, that's fine, just thought I could...

*(Silence.* **MAGGIE** *looks at the office door, then at* **BILLY***.)*

**MAGGIE**. Billy, I –...

*(She falters.)*

I can't do it.

*(Pause.)*

I – don't think I can go with you, Billy.

*(Pause.)*

**BILLY**. Oh, I –... Maggie, if I'm moving too fast, that's –

**MAGGIE**. I'm not coming, Billy.

*(Pause.)*

I'm not moving down there.

*(She goes to the register area, busying herself with arranging, cleaning.)*

**BILLY**. Maggie, what the hell is / going on?

**MAGGIE**. I'm sixty-five years old, Billy, I can't pretend like I'm twenty, I can't start over.

**BILLY**. I know it's a big decision, but I can help you with the move, that's what I'm saying –

**MAGGIE**. *(Curt.) It's a selfish idea. We're being selfish, Billy.*

> *(**BILLY** stares at her in silence. Finally, **MAGGIE** moves toward the front door, flipping the sign from "closed" to "open.")*

It was nice seeing you, I'm glad you made the trip. But this isn't gonna work out the way we want it to, so you and Kel should just go.

> *(She goes behind the register, not looking at **BILLY**.)*

> *(Silence.)*

**BILLY**. Are you scared?

> *(No response.)*

If you think I'm not scared, well then let me tell you something. I'm *terrified*. I spent all night rolling it all around in my head, wondering if this is the right thing, wondering if Joe is gonna be okay, what Kel will do when I'm gone, whether or not I'm just inviting you down there to watch me die.

> *(Short pause.)*

But then I really thought about it. I thought about this with sixty-four years behind me, and I'm realizing – every time I've been up against something like this in my life, I take the path of least resistance. When my mom wanted me to marry Sue, I thought – just give it time and you'll take to each other. When people were telling me that I had to confront Patrick about his drinking, I said he'll change, you just gotta give it time. And it's not until right now, right here, when I don't have any time to give, that I can't just –!

*(Suddenly,* **MONA** – *a bright, somewhat fashionable young woman* – *breezes in through the front door. She stops when she sees* **MAGGIE** *and* **BILLY**. **BILLY** *turns and sees her.)*

**MONA.** Oh, sorry! Are you open? I thought online it said nine?

*(Pause.* **BILLY** *looks back at* **MAGGIE**. **MAGGIE** *looks at* **BILLY** *for a brief moment, then turns away from him, going to* **MONA**.*)*

**MAGGIE.** Yeah, we –. We're open.

*(Pause.* **MONA** *senses the awkward tension in the room.* **BILLY** *keeps his eyes fixed on* **MAGGIE**, **MAGGIE** *doesn't look back at him.)*

**MONA.** Am I –...? I can come back –

**MAGGIE.** No, no. You're fine.

**MONA.** I'm just wondering – do you have any tickets left for the mine tour today?

**MAGGIE.** We actually... We don't do those anymore. Shutting down.

**MONA.** Oh really? Oh, that's so sad.

*(***BILLY** *keeps his eyes on* **MAGGIE**, **MAGGIE** *doesn't look back. Finally,* **BILLY** *starts making his way toward the front door, very slowly.)*

So is the museum shutting down as well?

**MAGGIE.** Today's our last day.

**MONA.** Your last day?! Oh my God, that's crazy! I'm so glad I came here today, then!

*(***BILLY** *is at the front door. He looks back at* **MAGGIE** *one last time.* **MAGGIE** *finally looks back at him.)*

*(***MONA** *starts looking around at some of the exhibits, maps, etc.)*

**MONA.** Are there any other companies in the area that do tours of the Dodson Mine?

(**BILLY** *and* **MAGGIE** *stare at one another. Pause.*)

(*Finally,* **MAGGIE** *shakes her head slightly, looking away from* **BILLY.** **BILLY** *turns and exits.*)

(**MONA** *looks at* **MAGGIE.**)

Ma'am?

(*Pause.* **MAGGIE** *looks at* **MONA.**)

I was just wondering if there were any other companies that do mine tours.

**MAGGIE.** No, we... Now that we're not a town anymore, no one's allowed down there.

**MONA.** You're kidding. God, it just keeps getting worse. It's just so stupid, it's criminal. So that's why you have to shut down now? It's just so sad. God, it's so sad. So what's going to happen to this place? Please tell me it's not going to get boarded up like everything else around here.

(*Pause.*)

**MAGGIE.** I live upstairs.

(**MONA** *looks at* **MAGGIE.**)

**MONA.** You *live* here? That's so neat!

(*She pauses, looking at* **MAGGIE.** **MAGGIE** *is paralyzed.*)

You know, I actually – I think I remember you.

(*Pause.* **MAGGIE** *looks at her.*)

Oh my God, I *do* remember you! That's so crazy, that was *decades* ago... And you used to take your son with you on the tours, right? He was so cute, probably like five or six years old...? That was your son, right?

(*Pause.*)

**MAGGIE**. Yeah.

**MONA**. He was so cute. Wait – he had a joke. I did the mine tour every summer, he'd tell the same joke every time, right? It was like – like someone falls down the mine, and then his boss says like, "Are you hurt?" I don't remember...

> *(Pause.)*

**MAGGIE**. Guy falls down into the mine. His boss yells at him, "Did you break anything?"

**MONA**. Yes!

**MAGGIE**. Guy shouts back, "Only rocks down here, sir, not much to break."

**MONA**. Right!

> *(Just then, she sees the pocket watch on the shelf above the counter.)*

That's so funny, I have such a specific memory of that thing, I always thought it was so cool. Do you mind if I –?

> *(She reaches up and takes the pocket watch, looking at it.)*

It's *amazing*, for some reason this thing sticks out in my memory so vividly.

> *(Pause.)*

**MAGGIE**. You can have it.

> *(**MONA** looks at **MAGGIE**.)*

We're closing up, I'm trying to get rid of everything. It's just some broken old watch.

**MONA**. Oh, I – I can't just *take* this from you –

**MAGGIE**. It's yours. Take it.

**MONA**. Well, I can't –. Let me give you something for it.

> *(She opens her purse.)*

**MAGGIE**. You don't need / to –

**MONA**. Just twenty dollars? Seriously, you'll make me feel better. Just twenty dollars, it's nothing.

*(Pause. Finally* **MAGGIE** *relents, takes the money. She goes to the register, opening it up.* **MONA** *looks at the watch.)*

**MONA**. It's the weirdest little things that stick with you, isn't it?

*(Pause.)*

My parents would take my sister and me to Clements, every summer, until they split up when I was eleven. I think I liked it because my parents wouldn't fight when they were here. Once we got back to California it all started back up again, but when we were here...

*(Pause.)*

My husband surprised me last Christmas by buying a few acres on the lake here. I was so excited to do everything that I did when I was a kid. But when I looked around town, I was shocked to see how much had changed. How much was gone.

*(She puts the pocket watch in her purse. She smiles at* **MAGGIE**.*)*

So anyway, it's just nice to come here and see at least *one* thing lasted. I'm so glad you're staying here, that at least *you'll* still be here. It really warms my heart.

*(She smiles at* **MAGGIE**.*)*

*(Then, suddenly,* **MAGGIE** *starts to break down, convulsing, doubling over on herself.* **MONA** *is shocked.)*

Oh – Oh, my –

*(She goes to* **MAGGIE**, *putting a hand on her back.)*

Oh my God, I'm so sorry, I'm just going on like a... Here.

*(She leads* **MAGGIE** *to a chair.* **MAGGIE** *remains hunched over.)*

I'm being so insensitive. Here I am going on and on about me, meanwhile you just lost your whole town, you're losing your business.

*(Pause. She rubs* **MAGGIE**'s *back.* **MAGGIE** *remains hunched over.)*

*(Finally:)*

**MAGGIE**. *(Small.)* I don't know what to do.

*(Pause.)*

I don't know what to do.

*(Silence.* **MONA** *thinks.)*

**MONA**. I know what you're feeling. I feel it too. We live in – scary times. Sometimes when I think about where we're headed, what it's going to be like when my kids are my age, your age…

*(Pause.)*

But then I just say to myself – you're going to be fine.

*(Short pause.)*

Hey.

*(Pause.* **MAGGIE** *lifts her head up, looking at* **MONA**. **MONA** *smiles at her warmly.)*

We're all going to be *fine*.

*(***MAGGIE** *looks at her.)*

*(Blackout.)*

**End of Play**